CODE NAME PIGEON

CODE NAME PIGEON

Book 5: Extraction

A Novel

Girad Clacy

iUniverse, Inc.
New York Bloomington

Code Name Pigeon
Book 5: Extraction

iUniverse books may be ordered through booksellers or by contacting:

iUniverse
1663 Liberty Drive
Bloomington, IN 47403
www.iuniverse.com
1-800-Authors (1-800-288-4677)

ISBN: 978-1-4401-3072-4 (pbk)
ISBN: 978-1-4401-3073-1 (ebk)

Printed in the United States of America

iUniverse rev. date: 3/9/2009

"I think I'm finally getting close to the end!"
I don't know who said this, but it sure seems to fit for this book.

SPOT Agent Michael Pigeon

CHAPTER 1

▼

Michael, still recovering from the injuries sustained during the last mission he went on, was resting comfortably when the phone rang. Michael thought everyone at the office knew that he was on Medical Leave Orders for at least another two weeks. He rolled his eyes a little and then reached over to grab the receiver. He put the receiver up to his ear and heard Bill's secretary on the other end.

"Michael Pigeon, are you there?" she asked nervously.

Michael noticed that she sounded rattled, almost frightened. Michael narrowed his eyes a little, from the pain he was in, more than anything else.

"Yes, I am. What can I do for you?"

"How soon before you can get to the office?"

"I'm trying to get some rest. What's going on, anyways?"

"I have the Director of the Central Intelligence Agency and four other CIA people in the office. They want to talk to you and they say it is urgent."

"All right, don't panic. I will get to the office in about 45 minutes, please ask them to wait."

"I will."

The line went dead. Michael pulled himself to the upright position and winced when he tried to stand up. The bone fusions that the military medical surgeons had used, to fix his left arm and right leg, still hurt whenever he put any amount of weight on the injury.

He shuffled over to the closet and used his right arm to pull some clothes out. He was able to get himself dressed. In a short while, he was downtown on the Light Rail System and was walking through the outer office doors. He looked at Bill's secretary.

"They're waiting for you, Mr. Pigeon," she said.

"Is it really the Director of the CIA or is it someone who represents the CIA?"

"The badge and identification he showed me said that he was really the director."

"I wonder what they want," said Michael, as he opened up the double doors and headed into Bill's office.

When he stepped into the office, one of the four persons standing in the room walked over and shut the doors for Michael. That same person then locked the doors. Michael looked over the men standing in the room.

The first one to his left was indeed the Director of the CIA, Roger Smith. Michael had seen his picture many times before. The man standing to the director's right was the Assistant Director of the CIA, Marcos Sanchez. Michael recognized the man standing to his right as the Chief of Intelligence, Jonathan Greer at the CIA. The other man Michael knew as the Chief of Counter-Terrorism, Nathanial, or Nate as everyone else called him, Kozee. The Director of the CIA spoke first.

"Mr. Pigeon, do you know who I am?"

"Yes, sir. You're the Director of the Central Intelligence Agency which is part of the Department of Homeland Security," replied Michael, confidently.

"Very good. Do you recognize any of the other personnel in this room?"

"Yes, sir. Your assistants are here, Jonathan Greer and Nate Kozee."

"Very good. Michael, why don't you have a seat," said the director.

"Okay," replied Michael, taking up a seat that was near the window.

Once Michael had sat down in the seat, he kept a careful eye on everyone. The CIA director spoke once again.

"Michael, how much do you know about Bill's trip?"

"He told me that he was going along as escort and moral support for the newly elected Secretary of State Everett."

"Good. Do you know where they were going?"

"Not exactly. Bill gave me a brief rundown on the situation and told me that the trip involved visiting countries that support terrorism. I think the goal might have been to persuade these other countries that supporting terrorism wasn't a good idea."

"Excellent. Now, what I'm about to tell you is probably going to come as a shock to you. Bill left specific instructions with me that I was to get a hold of you if something happened to him."

"Did something happen to him?" asked Michael, now very much alarmed.

"Yes. Sometime yesterday evening, the plane that Bill and those other diplomats were on, disappeared off of the radar screen while flying over some unfriendly territory," said John Greer.

"Did they crash?"

"We don't think so," replied John Greer.

"What evidence do you have to support that claim?" asked Michael.

"We have had satellites fly over their flight path and take pictures. So far, none of those pictures shows the wreckage of the plane," replied the chief once again.

"Then maybe they're alive. Have you picked up their emergency signal?"

"No. There's more to this than what Bill told you," said Nathan Kozee.

"What's that, sir?" asked Michael, although he almost knew what the answer would be anyway.

"Bill, Everett and those diplomats were also gathering intelligence for us for future cruise missile attacks, if needed," said the counterterrorism chief.

"What's the problem, then? I mean, you've got special teams for this, right Mr. Director?"

"Yes and no. Yes, I do have special teams for rescue missions, but no I don't have any ready to go yet," replied the director.

"Why not?"

"Remember, their plane flew through some unfriendly airspace and there is a possibility that they were either forced to land or they were shot down," said the intelligence chief.

"You mean to tell me as the Central Intelligence Agency, that you don't know what happened?"

"That's right, Mr. Pigeon."

"In fact, Mr. Pigeon, on the probable countries that their plane could have landed in, we have no intelligence on them," said the counterterrorism chief.

"Wait a minute, you mean to tell me that the Central Intelligence Agency has no intelligence on these countries?"

"Nothing beyond rudimentary information," replied the intelligence chief.

"Oh, now, that's just great. What do I have to do with all of this?"

"Bill always believed in you. He said you had great abilities to accomplish things and that you were very creative at times. I have researched your missions that you have been on and know that statement is true," said the director.

"I'm glad Bill thinks I'm great. I'm still healing up from a previous mission that almost got me killed."

"I am aware of that, Mr. Pigeon. However, Bill specifically left instructions that if anything happened to him on this trip, you were to be called immediately," said the director.

"In other words, I'm going in on an extraction mission?"

"Yes, sir, in theory. My intelligence chief here will brief you this afternoon at 1300 hours in conference room six," said the director.

"I'll be here," said Michael.

Michael pulled himself up out of the chair and winced once again. He slowly walked over to the double doors and waited for the intelligence chief to unlock them.

Once they were unlocked, Michael left the office and went to see the SPOT Unit doctor. He walked uneasily into the office as the secretary looked up, saw who it was and motioned him into one of the exam rooms. The doctor showed up a little while later.

"Sorry about the delay, Michael, what can I do for you?" asked the doctor.

"Am I well enough to take on a mission?"

"Let me see," said the doctor, as he reviewed Michael's medical charts.

The doctor looked over them for about five minutes and then

looked up at Michael. The doctor could see the pain that he was in and thought it probably wasn't a good idea to be going anywhere for a little while longer.

"No, Michael, I don't think you can go on a mission. You're exterior wounds are healed, but deep inside, you may not be healed yet. Your lung capacity tests are below the minimum acceptable standards as well. Does someone want you to go on a mission?"

"Yes."

"Who?"

"The Director of the CIA."

"I see. Let me tell you what. I can arrange for a bone density scan of those repaired areas. If the bone density scan shows that the bones are within the minimum limits, I can let you go on the mission, if not, I will ground you."

"I have to go on this mission."

"Why?"

"It's a personal thing. It's Bill, some diplomats, probably from the UN and Secretary of State Everett."

"I see. Well, I will see you in three days for the bone density scan. I suggest that you start taking Calcium tablets starting today at double their recommended dosage levels."

"Yes, sir."

Michael left the doctor's office and went home for lunch. After lunch and taking four chewable Calcium tablets, he returned back to work. He walked down the hallway to conference room six. He opened the door and walked inside, taking a seat in the middle of the conference room.

The seat faced the large screen that hung down. He looked down at the table and saw Jonathan Greer and Nate Kozee were seated. The intelligence chief stood up and the lights dimmed. A picture of the diplomats and their flight path appeared on the screen.

"As you can see, Mr. Pigeon, their flight path took them across these unfriendly nations marked in red outlines on the map," started John Greer.

"What kind of an aircraft were they flying in?" asked Michael.

"A chartered, government Boeing 767-400C series aircraft," replied John.

A picture of the civilian jetliner showed up on the screen and was rotated around a few times before disappearing. John went on with his speech.

"We lost radar contact at this point here," said John, pointing to the airspace of the outermost unfriendly nation.

"How much fuel did they have on board?"

"We don't know. If the fuel tanks were full, then the plane could have landed anywhere in this area," replied John, making a small circle around the other unfriendly nations.

"In other words, those diplomats, which I surmise are probably from the United Nations, Bill and Secretary of State Everett are probably hostages?" asked Michael.

"That is a definite possibility. However, they may be imprisoned while the plane is used for transportation by any one of those nations," said Nathan.

"Any ransom requests?"

"None so far," said John.

"What information do you have about those countries?"

"We know what form of government they are, we know their population, economics structure and a few other things. However we don't know what kind of a military structure they have," said Nathan.

"Do any of those countries have fighter jets?"

"All of them. However, they are older F-4 Phantoms and some MiG-29's," replied Nathan.

"How many of those countries have an airstrip capable of handling a 767?"

"Again, all of them," replied John.

"You mean to tell me that these countries all have paved runways that are at least 2,000 meters long?"

"No, in fact, out of those countries, almost all of them have dirt runways. Why?" asked Nathan.

"The Boeing 737 is the only plane that can land and take off from a hard packed dirt or gravel runway. All other aircraft require paved runways."

"That's interesting, Mr. Pigeon. Will you please excuse me, John, I have to make a phone call," said Nathan, as he hurriedly exited the conference room.

After the doors had shut to the conference room, John went on with the briefing.

"Are you currently medically able to take on this mission?" asked John.

"I have a final bone density scan in three days. I am also scheduled to have another lung capacity test series completed. If those tests come back okay, then, yes, I can go. Otherwise, I cannot."

"They have enough food and water to last them six days. That doesn't give us much time."

"I understand, sir. Is there any way I can get the intelligence on these countries and take it home to read?"

"I can give you a copy of it. Make sure that it doesn't fall into the wrong hands, if you know what I mean."

"I know what you mean."

"Let us know about the tests by Friday."

"Yes, sir."

Michael departed the conference room and was handed the printouts on the foreign unfriendly nations. He went home to rest some more. After taking off his clothes and taking a shower, he sat down in the living room on his couch to read the printouts. The printouts were very informative from Michael's point of view.

By early morning, he had finished reading about those nations. He had just crawled into bed when the phone rang. He looked at the time on the clock; it was 0145 hours on a Saturday morning. Groggily, he picked up the receiver.

"Michael, this is Nathan, I have some good and bad news for you," said Nathan.

Michael tried sitting up in bed but decided to just roll over instead. He winced a little as he rolled over onto his left arm. He suddenly sat straight up in bed.

"Well, at this point in time, any news is better than no news," replied Michael.

"I had my research staff use satellites to look at all those foreign countries' airports and runways. There are many of them that are paved, however, I asked our staff to narrow it down to the airports whose runways are more than 2,000 meters in length."

"I'm very impressed, Nathan, that you caught onto my request for information," said Michael.

"Hey, I'm in counterterrorism and I did counterintelligence for a number of years."

"What did you find?"

"Out of those foreign unfriendly nations, a total of 75 airstrips were found by satellites. I was able to narrow the list down to 10 with paved runways of more than 2,000 meters in length."

"Well, that was certainly worth the call in the middle of the night."

"I'm sorry that I couldn't narrow it down any further."

"Well, actually you have. Could you fax the list to Bill's office? Then could you send the flight plans and last known flight path to Bill's office so that I could take a look at it later on this morning?"

"Not a problem, Michael. If anything else comes up, I will let you know."

"Thank you."

After Michael hung up the phone, he rolled back over and slept for another hour. He woke up to the sound of someone trying to break into his apartment. Carefully he stepped out of bed and grabbed his .357 magnum revolver off the nightstand. He approached the door with caution, cocked back the hammer and waited.

The door came flying open and two men in ski masks jumped into the living room. Not expecting to find Michael, the homeowner, home, they both stopped in their tracks. Michael shot the first one and then moved to the second one. Both were on the floor withering around before becoming silent. As Michael moved towards the phone, one of them stretched out their left leg and tripped him. Michael hit the floor and passed out.

When he woke up, the both of them were gone. His revolver was still in his right hand. He used the cabinets in the kitchen to pull himself to an upright position. After regaining his senses, he picked up the phone in the kitchen and called 911.

Within minutes, the Denver Police Department and an ambulance were at his place along with SPOT personnel. The police questioned Michael and then let him go with the SPOT personnel to the hospital. At the hospital, Michael was treated and released.

When Michael arrived back at his apartment, he noticed someone had locked his door. He was lucky that he had remembered the key before he left. Once he was inside, he called his flight instructor.

"Hello Michael, it's been awhile. What's going on?"

"Heavy stuff with the government, you know."

"Yeah, I know."

"How hard would it be to fly a Boeing 767-400C series airplane?"

"Not hard at all. In fact, that model of aircraft is very advanced."

"How long would it take to learn to fly one?"

"About 2,000 flying hours in a simulator per FAA regulations. However, if you can fly those twin engine aircraft, there's nothing different there except for the amount of hydraulics and gauges."

"That's great to know, goodbye."

Michael hung up the phone and turned on his computer. He inserted a computer disc into the disc slot and started learning how to fly the Boeing 737 aircraft. After many crashes on both landing and takeoff, he finally mastered the controls and noticed how similar they were to the little planes he was flying.

Michael also noticed that although there were lots of other controls and gauges, the plane did handle exactly the same way as the little ones he was already flying. After lunch, Michael went to the building and picked up the faxes that had been sent to him. From there, he drove out to the airfield.

Once he was out at the airfield, he took the information he had into a small room and started flipping through the air charts. He finally found three air charts for the respective countries. He then picked up a black grease pencil from the chart-table and started drawing lines. Some of the lines were dark and he had marked them as a "known flight path."

Other lines were either dotted or dashed and marked as "Probable or possible flight path." He took those calculations and saw that there were indeed at least 10 airfields that could handle the aircraft. Now, all he had to do was find out which one had the plane. He left there and headed back home for some more rest.

He arrived at home, took some more Calcium tablets and sat down on the edge of the bed. As he was reviewing the information in his head once again, a thought hit him. He walked out of the bedroom and into the kitchen.

He then called Nathan and asked him for some specific information. Nathan said he would send the information in the morning. Michael hung up the phone and went to bed. During the night, the only dreams Michael had were of the two masked men who broke into his apartment and of Bill, the diplomats and Everett. Michael had nightmares for the rest of the night.

He woke up the next morning just before daybreak. He felt something wet touch his hands, he looked down to discover that the bed sheets were soaked with his sweat from the nightmares. Getting up, he took a shower before going into work.

CHAPTER 2

▼

Michael drove to work that morning. As he arrived at work, he went immediately to the medical exam room. The nurse informed Michael that the doctor wouldn't be in today until later on in the afternoon. She then handed Michael a stack of orders to take to the hospital.

He left there and went to the hospital, checking into the waiting area for Magnetic Resonance Imaging or the MRI as most people called it. The nurse there took his paperwork and told him to have a seat. As Michael waited for his MRI, the Director of the CIA and Jonathan Greer were having breakfast not too far from him. As the Director stirred his coffee, he looked across the table at the Intelligence Chief.

"We must have another plan ready to go in case the good doctor doesn't let Michael go on this mission," said the Chief, as he took a sip of coffee.

The Director had just finished stirring his coffee and had set the spoon down on the tabletop as he looked up into the Chief's eyes.

"If the good doctor doesn't let Michael go on the mission, then we have no other plan and those good people are going to die," replied the director, as he sipped his coffee.

"I don't want that to happen. What must we do to ensure that Michael goes on the mission?" asked the Chief.

"Everybody has their price in this world. Find out what the good doctor's is and use it against him," replied the Director.

"I understand. I will accomplish the mission one way or the other," said the Chief as he finished off his coffee and paid for the breakfast.

Meanwhile, Michael had finally been called into the MRI area of the hospital. The nurse instructed Michael to take off his clothes and put on the hospital gown that was in the room. Michael did this and stepped back out as the nurse was going into a booth directly in front of the MRI machine. She was typing up something when Michael came from around the corner. She looked up and came out from the booth.

"Mr. Pigeon, if you will lie down on the table, we will get started. Here is your ear protection," she said.

"Thank you," he replied, taking the earplugs and putting them inside his ears.

He laid himself down on the table and with the help of the nurse, he was able to get positioned right. The nurse left him and went back into the booth. She started typing once again and the MRI machine came to life. Michael was moved into the machine and the loud banging started once again.

In what seemed like a few minutes instead of hours, Michael was pulled out of the machine. He stood up from the table and stepped off the table onto the floor. The nurse came out of the booth and was smiling.

"Am I done?" asked Michael handing over the earplugs.

"Yes. The results will be interpreted by our Chief Radiologist and the Head of Orthopedic Surgery."

"When will the results be ready?"

"In a few minutes, but it could be next week before the doctors all get around to interpreting the results and provide those results to your doctor."

"Thank you."

Michael dressed and headed back to work. He stopped in to see the doctor and found out that the doctor was in a conference with some people. He told the nurse to let the doctor know that he had completed the MRI. She agreed to tell the doctor the news. Michael then went up to the eighth floor and found no one in Bill's office. Michael spoke to Bill's secretary.

"Any word from Bill or the others?" asked Michael.

"None. Those CIA guys make me nervous," she said.

"I know what you mean. Any messages for me?"

"Only one. The Counterterrorism guy, Mr. Kozee, said that he sent the information you requested via video link to here. He said you would know what to do with the information."

"Thank you."

Michael left the office and went to conference room six. He walked into the room and turned on the lights. He then locked both sets of double-doors to the conference room. Michael then proceeded to locate the information that was on the video link.

He found the video link button and activated the video screen that soon dropped behind him. As he took a seat in the middle of the room, he made himself comfortable. The voice that came over the speaker system was Nate Kozee's.

"Good day to you, Michael. Here is the information you requested."

A picture soon appeared and showed the radarscope images that Michael had asked for. He noticed nothing out of the ordinary until he looked at the images to the right and left side of the airplane. Michael saw two small images and stopped the video link temporarily. Next, he backed up the video link and found a keyboard under the table in the front of the room.

He used the joystick type control on the far right side of the keyboard to move around a small curser. After placing the curser on the images, he froze them on the screen and then printed them up. After this was done, he went back to the video link presentation.

"As you can see, Michael, Bill, Everett and the others are probably in this unfriendly nation, as I will call it. We know very little about this nation except that it is very religiously run. Their laws seem to be centered on religious values. Their current form of government seems to be some kind of a dictatorship. Beyond that, we have no new information," said Nate.

Michael stood up and turned off the video link. He walked over to the printer and extracted the two images. He then unlocked the doors, turned off the lights and went up to the eighth floor. He found the number for the Counterterrorism Chief and called him at Langley, Virginia.

"Hello, Michael, what can I do for you?" asked Nate.

"I have two unidentified images that I want to fax to you for analysis," replied Michael.

"Sure, please send them on the secure fax line."

"Will do. Let me know what those unidentified images are as soon as possible, please."

"I will try and get them back to you in less than 24 hours."

"I'll send them today,"

Michael hung up the phone and went into Bill's office. He placed the images into the fax machine and pressed the little red button on top of the fax machine to obtain a secure line. Once the secure line had been established, he scanned the images into the fax machine and pressed the "send" button. After this was done, he put the images into the shred bin in Bill's office and walked back out the door. Michael went home for the day.

The next morning dawned clear and cold. Michael woke up, ate his Calcium tablets and went into the kitchen to fix him something to eat. As he was eating his breakfast, Michael couldn't help but think where Bill and Everett where at and what was happening to them. He kept looking at the phone in the kitchen as he finished off his breakfast. The phone rang and Michael answered it quickly.

"Michael, this is Nate. I have the answer to the question you sent me. However, without a secure line, I cannot reveal the nature of the answer to you," said Nate.

"I understand. Is there anything else you have found out that you can tell me right now?"

"Yes, the grounds crew at Cairo, Egypt International Airport reported that they fully fueled the plane before it took off. They also fully resupplied the plane as well."

"That's good news. I will be arriving at Bill's office sometime in the next hour. I will call you on his secure phone from there."

"Very well, I will be awaiting your call."

Michael hung up the phone and dressed. He put on something warm and then drove into work. After parking the car, he walked up a few flights of stairs before he became exhausted and had to exit the stairs to use the elevator. He walked with a slight limp over to the elevator and pushed the call button.

In a few minutes the elevator doors opened and Michael was soon walking into Bill's office. Michael shut the double-doors and locked them. Next, he sat in Bill's office chair and picked up the secure phone on Bill's desk. He then dialed the number to Nate's office.

"Hello, Nate, I am on a secure line now," said Michael.

"Good. Those images were verified by a radar operator in the Air Force out here at Vandenberg Air Force Base as the radar signatures of Mig-29's."

"Mig-29's, aren't those short-range fighters?"

"Yes, I believe they are. But they can have extended ranges with external fuel tanks attached to them; why?"

"Nate, tell me how many of those 10 airfields were within those Mig-29's flight capacities."

"Can I call you back?"

"Sure."

Michael hung up the phone and could only wait now for the information to come back.

Meanwhile, the test results had come back to the doctor. The doctor looked at the results and then looked at the average bone mass density. The doctor wanted at least a 5.5 density reading in order to let Michael go on the mission. As he went to call Bill's secretary to have Michael come in for a chat about his test results, he looked up to see the CIA Intelligence Chief standing in his office.

"What can I do for you?" asked the doctor.

"Do you have Michael Pigeon's results back yet?"

"Yes, but I cannot give you the test results per HIPAA standards."

"I'm not interested in that kind of information. I want to know if he can go on a mission, doctor."

"No, he cannot go on a mission. At least not now; maybe in a few months."

"Why can he not go on a mission?"

"Bone mass density scan was not within acceptable limits. Also, his lung capacity tests were not within the minimum acceptable standards."

"What are the acceptable limits?"

"5.5 on the bone mass index scale and at least 80 percent on the lung capacity tests."

"And his is not even close to those limits?"

"No."

"How far off?"

".3 off on the bone mass density scan and his lung capacity tests were at only 77 percent."

"I see. We need him to go on a mission as soon as possible."

"I cannot allow him to go on a mission. I cannot let him take the risk of breaking those bones again and being in worse condition than he is now."

"Doctor, as far as you're concerned, Michael Pigeon is fit for duty as of now."

"I don't believe it, you're asking me to put someone's life in danger."

"My good doctor, many lives are in danger at this time. I don't have enough time to put together a good extraction unit. Bill Yancy gave high marks to Mr. Pigeon. Now, let's find him fit for duty."

"Are you trying to bribe me?"

"If you want to call it that, then, yes. My good doctor, you owe your medical school $179,500.00 in school monies."

"What are you saying?"

"It's going to take you the rest of your life to pay that amount of money off, unless you find a mysterious benefactor."

"What?!"

"Listen, you scratch my back, I'll scratch yours. You find Michael fit for duty and I'll make sure that you never receive another bill for medical school costs again."

"I see what you're saying. Okay, I'll find Michael fit for duty."

"And I will make sure that your medical school bills are paid off; thank you doctor, you have been most accommodating."

As Jonathan Greer left the room to make the arrangements to pay off the doctor's medical school bills, the doctor went about writing up the appropriate paperwork to find Michael fit for duty. He finished off the paperwork and left it sitting up front with his nurse.

He told his nurse that he was leaving for the day. She looked in Michael's medical record and found his cell phone number. She called it and left a message that he was to come to the doctor's office to obtain his fit for duty paperwork. Michael showed up a few hours later to pick up the paperwork. As he left the doctor's office, he headed out to the airfield to see his flight instructor. Michael walked into the flight instructor's office.

"I feel confident enough to take on the flight simulator," said Michael.

"Okay. Let's walk across the airfield to that small structure to the left of the tower," replied his flight instructor.

They walked across the airfield and into the small structure. Once they were inside the structure, the instructor turned Michael over to a young woman who was going to teach Michael to fly the 737 simulator. After a brief ground school of about three hours, Michael was put into the simulator.

He discovered that the simulator was very much different from the computer screen that he had been practicing on at his apartment. The flight instructor closed the door and started the simulation. Michael left there after a few more hours and several "crashes", feeling very low on confidence that he could fly a plane like that if the need arose.

Meanwhile, the Director of the CIA and Jonathan Greer were having another meeting. This time it was at a different location and they had invited Nate Kozee to be there as well. As the men all sat down, they started looking over the menu and then ordered their meals. They ate their meals in silence until finally the Director of the CIA spoke first.

"Did you accomplish the mission?" he asked as he stared at Jonathan Greer.

"Yes, sir, I did. The good doctor was most obliging. The only thing you have to do is sign the check," he replied sarcastically.

"In other words, you bought him off?"

"Not exactly, I impressed upon him the urgency of this mission and the fact that he owed money for his medical school bills. I agreed to pay off the medical school bills and he agreed to find Michael fit for duty."

"I am most impressed with your high degree of creativity."

"Thank you, sir."

"Has Michael asked for any more information recently?" asked the Director, showing an interest in Nate Kozee.

"Yes, he has asked for some unusual information. Per your orders, I have complied with his requests and gave him the information."

"Good, keep the information flowing to him."

"I will. Now, who's going to pay for dinner?"

"I will," said the Director, pulling out a couple of $100 bills, leaving one on the table with the bill. He put the other into his front suit jacket pocket for the taxi driver.

They all left the restaurant and went their separate ways. The Counterterrorism Chief went to the airport to catch the late night flight back to Washington, D.C. The Director and the Intelligence Chief went back to their hotel rooms. They discussed further plans of what they wanted out of Michael before going to sleep.

Michael was tossing and turning in his sleep once again. He saw the same faces and woke up breathing fast and shallow along with the sweat soaked sheets. He stepped out of bed and walked into the bathroom and took another shower. After he was finished with the shower, he was getting back into bed when the phone rang. Michael walked into the kitchen to answer the phone.

"Hello?" asked Michael.

"Is Michael Pigeon there?" asked a voice that Michael did not recognize.

"Yes, this is Michael Pigeon."

"You have a call from the country of Lenora. To accept this call, press 1."

Michael took the receiver away from his ear and pressed the 1 key. Soon, the same voice said something else to Michael as he put the phone back up to his ear.

"Thank you for using International Watts Lines."

Michael heard silence before a frantic message was played for him. He thought he could make out the sound of a gunshot before the message ended. He hoped that the message would playback again. Patiently, Michael waited until the message repeated before he determined that the message was from Everett. Michael started to write down everything she said.

"Michael, I can't talk long because they probably have detected this outgoing message. We are okay for right now; I am unharmed but we are in this strange place. I don't know the country's name, but we are in the desert; look in the desert," she said as she hung up. The noise at the end, Michael determined was probably the phone being hung up.

Michael went back to bed and thought that all of this was nothing more than a crazy nightmare that needed to end soon. He had just closed his eyes when the alarm clock went off. He woke up and started getting dressed once again for a cold, but overcast, day. He fixed himself some breakfast and then went into work to see if anyone had heard from Bill, Everett or the persons who forced their plane to land.

He arrived at work, checked with Bill's replacement secretary for anything new and then went out to the airfield once again. This time he was determined more than ever to learn how to fly the simulator. He was able to land several times before lunch without "crashing."

This boosted his confidence level and when he returned from lunch, the flight instructor started showing him what to do during emergencies. He didn't do well with emergencies, but still, he was determined to do better the next time. As he was leaving the airfield, he received a phone call on his cell phone from Jonathan Greer.

"Yes, sir, what can I do for you?" asked Michael.

"When you are ready, we have prepared a mission briefing."

"Sounds good to me. Say, was one of those unfriendly nations called Lenora?"

"Yes, that name is correct. How did you find out about that country?" asked the chief, expressing a keen interest in the conversation now.

"I received a very strange message early this morning from the country of Lenora. A mechanical voice called the message an International Watts Line."

"Michael, that message from the International Watts Line was from Everett's emergency cell phone. Michael, do I have your permission to trace that phone call?"

"Sure. I still think it is a hoax,"

"Well, I don't think so. In fact, I think you have the most accurate information available. Be talking to you soon."

"Goodbye."

Michael hung up his phone and went back to his apartment. He changed clothes and ate some dinner. When he had finished dinner, he closed his eyes for a few minutes to rest them and that's when the phone rang.

CHAPTER 3

▼

The Intelligence Chief acted on the information. He obtained a seizure warrant from a federal judge in Washington, D.C. and served the warrant on the phone company who held Michael's phone records. The information was confirmed within an hour that the call did indeed come from Everett's cell phone.

The call was confirmed as having come through multiple relay stations in Africa, the Middle East and Europe before arriving in the United States. The chief took this information and called the Director in Denver. The Director was in conference room six with Michael. The Director didn't want to be bothered, but thought that the nature of the phone call was important enough to stop the mission briefing.

"What is it that you want?" snapped the Director.

"Michael was contacted by Everett early yesterday morning," replied the Intelligence Chief.

"What evidence do you have to support this statement?"

"I was able to obtain verbal permission to access Michael's phone records. I was also able to secure a seizure warrant for his phone messages. I was able to verify that the message that Michael heard yesterday morning originated from the country of Lenora."

"So, that doesn't prove anything, it could have been a wrong number."

"The message that Michael heard was preceded by a mechanical voice that said 'thank you for using International Watts Line.'"

"Can you confirm the number?"

"No. She was only on the phone line for 19 seconds to leave the message for Michael. I'm washing the message through the computer to see if there is anything else on the message that is discernible."

"Good work. Let me know if anything else comes up."

"Yes, sir."

The Director walked back into the conference room and looked at Michael.

"Michael, I understand that you may have had contact with Everett?" he asked.

"Yes, I think I did yesterday morning. At first I thought it was some sort of hallucination."

"Well, according to the Intelligence Chief, it was not a hallucination. His computer personnel are checking the message for other clues."

"Oh, so it wasn't a figment of my imagination or some early morning nightmare."

"You've been having nightmares, Michael?"

"Yes, ever since those two guys in black ski masks broke into my apartment a few days ago. The police are looking for them, but I don't think they're anywhere near here."

"What makes you think that?"

"I shot both of them twice. A double-tap shot, as it is called, with my .357 magnum revolver. When I went to call for help, one of them tripped me and I fell onto the floor unconscious. When I woke up, they were gone."

"Michael, were you using .38 Special load by any chance?"

"Negative, I use .357 magnum load in the revolver."

"I see. What load was in the revolver that morning?"

"145 grain, Silvertip Hollow point® from Winchester."

"Where did you shoot them?"

"I thought that I had hit them center mass, but now, I'm not so sure."

"Michael, I'm going to send a special crime scene team over to your place right now. Don't leave this room."

"I won't."

The Director left the room and called his contact in Denver. The Denver office of the CIA responded quickly. They dusted for fingerprints but found none except Michael's. Then they sprayed the place down with Luminal®. The entire room lit up bright green.

Blood was all over the wall directly in front of where Michael had said he had shot the two men. One of the technicians put on his special glasses and grabbed a spray bottle and started spraying down the area outside Michael's apartment.

Within minutes, the technician, followed by two heavily armed CIA agents from the Denver field office, started following the blood trail that had been left by the two men. In a few minutes, the trail had led the group to the parking lot. There, the technician sprayed down the area where he lost the trail. Nothing showed up, so the technician made his report.

He then walked back into Michael's place and took samples of the blood to the mobile crime lab. Within minutes, the mobile crime lab was able to determine what the blood types were and what nationality they were. The technician read the report to the Intelligence Chief who then typed in the information into the computer and asked the computer to cross-reference the blood types.

The computer, able to calculate things much quicker than a human, was able to determine what possible geographic regions of the world the blood types were common to. In addition, the computer calculated what probable countries of origin the two men were. Next, the computer offered up a list of probable countries that those people could have come from.

Of those countries, three were on the terrorist hit list, Nigeria, Lenora and Ghana. The computer printed the probable lists and the Intelligence Chief sent them to the Denver field office via secure fax. The Director was standing there with Michael when the results of the computer's conclusions were finally printed up.

"Michael, did you notice anything peculiar about those two people?" asked the Director.

"No, not that I could remember, why?"

"Those two men were from Central Africa. In fact the computer cross-referenced their blood types to the countries of Nigeria, Lenora, and Ghana."

"And Lenora was where the mysterious phone call originated."

"Right. Now, until those men are caught or are found dead, you need to take better care of your personal security."

"Am I going to be babysat again?"

"Yes. I am going to make the arrangements starting now."

As the Director started to make the arrangements, Michael received a call on his cell phone. It was the Denver Police Department and the detective in charge of the shooting investigation wanted to talk to him. The detective left a number that Michael could call him back at. When Michael called the number, the switchboard operator transferred him to the detective.

"Michael, thank you for calling me back so soon. I need you to come down to the city morgue and see if the two men we recently received down here are the ones you shot."

"Yes, sir, I will be down there shortly."

"Look forward to seeing you."

Michael was hanging up the phone when the Director came back into the room. The Director was about to speak when Michael stopped him from talking.

"I don't think you will have to worry about the babysitting party," said Michael.

"Why?"

"I was just informed by the Denver Police Department detective who was assigned to my shooting case that there are two dead, as yet unidentified, bodies at the morgue. He wants me to come down and see if it's my handiwork."

"Okay, but remember you're movements are going to be watched carefully."

"I understand."

Michael walked out the door and walked down to his car. He stepped into his car and started the engine. He drove in silence to the city morgue. The place was dimly lighted and the overall feeling of the neighborhood was one of dread. He saw the unmarked police car and walked on up to the wooden door that marked the entrance to the morgue.

Michael opened the door and walked into the reception area. A young man stood up from behind the bulletproof glass and iron girder structure that was the office and turned on the microphone to speak to Michael.

"Yes, sir, what can I do for you?" he asked.

"I'm here to see Detective Carlos Sintara. He called me earlier and asked me to come down here."

"Yes, sir. What is your name?" asked the clerk, as he dialed the internal number to where the detective was.

"Michael Pigeon."

"Wait one moment."

The clerk turned off the microphone and spoke into the phone receiver. In a few minutes, the clerk returned back to Michael.

"Mr. Pigeon, please empty your pockets into the drawer and take off your shoes and belt if you are wearing one. Place these items into the drawer and proceed through the door and the detective will meet you there."

"Yes, sir."

Michael emptied his pockets and then took off both his belt and his shoes and placed them into the thick, metal drawer that was sticking out. Once he was done with all of this, Michael was buzzed through the two heavy glass and metal reinforced doors where he was allowed to have all of his stuff back. He had just finished putting on his shoes when the detective showed up in front of him.

"Good evening, Michael. Glad you could come down here. Now, before we step into the room with those two unidentified bodies, you did say you shot them at some where between 1.1 and 1.3 meters, correct?"

"Yes, sir."

"And you were shooting a .357 magnum revolver with .357 magnum, 145 grain, Silvertip Hollow Point® Winchester rounds, correct?"

"Yes, sir."

"Please step this way."

The detective lead Michael down the hallway to the last door on the end. The detective opened the door and showed Michael into the morgue. The morgue attendant, who was also the medical examiner, stood up from her desk. She then picked up the evidence bag containing two bullets. One was almost intact, while the other one was severely deformed.

"Mr. Pigeon, I understand that there is a possibility these two dead bodies might be your handiwork," she said.

"What makes you think that?" asked Michael, nervously.

"These bullets are 145 grain Silvertip Hollow Point® Winchester's that I recovered from the bodies. Indications are they came from a .357 magnum revolver, they were fired at close range, and they entered the bodies in two, quick, successive shots. I believe the term, I learned in police academy I took many years ago, is referred to as a double-tap."

"Well, then, let's take a look at these bodies."

"Right this way."

The bodies were pulled out of one of the many refrigerators. The medical examiner pulled back the sheets that were covering them and Michael saw their faces. Their faces told him they were possibly from Africa. He nodded his head and she closed them back up into the refrigerator.

"Are those the men, Mr. Pigeon?" asked the detective.

"I'm not for certain, but they look like it. I suggest that if you run their fingerprints through INTERPOL, you might find they are from Central Africa and quite possibly from the country of Lenora."

"Thank you, sir. You're dismissed."

As Michael was leaving, the detective picked up his printout and read it again. He then looked over at the medical examiner and shook his head. She looked back at the detective rather curiously.

"What's the matter detective?" she asked.

"How the hell did he know they were from Central Africa and, what's more, how the hell did he know they were from the country of Lenora?"

"Maybe he is psychic."

Michael called the Director and let him know that he could call off his babysitting triage. Michael went to Bill's office and sat down at Bill's computer. He turned it on and typed up his brief. He then faxed it over to where the Director was staying at all night.

Michael turned off the computer and went downstairs to go home. When he arrived at his apartment, he closed the door and double locked the front door. Then he went about setting up booby traps once again to alert him to anyone wandering around the place.

Michael sat down and noticed that the message light was flashing on his telephone. He walked over to the kitchen and picked up the receiver. He then dialed the phone number to retrieve messages and punched in his PIN number.

The message was from the Intelligence Chief. He needed Michael to call him back right away. Michael let the message finish and deleted the message. Michael then sat down on his couch and called the Intelligence Chief.

"Michael, I just got off the phone with the Director. I have the autopsy reports on your friends."

"Great, how bad of a shot was I?"

"A very good shot. In fact, one of them you shot, you punctured both lungs with that double-tap shooting."

"That would explain why that one dropped to the floor so quickly."

"Yes, it would. The other one was gravely wounded as well, however, you missed the heart by half an inch and the liver by a one-eighth of an inch."

"Well, guess I will have to practice my marksmanship in the dark."

"Sounds like a plan. By the way, I just find it a little too coincidental that those guys broke into your apartment."

"I was thinking the same thing."

"I don't want to second guess the Director, but be prepared to travel to the Country of Lenora and very soon."

"I'll start packing right now."

"Goodnight, sir and good luck."

Michael had just hung up the phone, when there came a knock on his door. Carefully, he moved to the front door and looked through the peephole to see who it was.

The Director and a whole collection of heavily armed personnel were standing in the hallway leading into his apartment. He unlocked both locks and opened the door. As the Director was stepping into Michael's apartment, he turned to the large man holding a 9mm automatic weapon known as an Uzi and spoke to him.

"Secure the perimeter and I don't want anything to get to Michael,"

"Yes, sir."

The man walked down the hallway and the other personnel scattered in all directions. The Director walked into the apartment and closed the door. Next, he locked both locks and then turned to face Michael.

"Michael, has the Intelligence Chief been in contact with you, say, within the last two hours?" asked the Director.

"Yes. He left a message for me to call him and when I did he said he had the autopsy results on those two dead bodies that were my handiwork as everyone likes to call it."

"I see. Has he called you any more recently than that?"

"No, sir."

"Well, he called me earlier today. His computer team had cleaned up the message that he retrieved from your telephone company. The message seems to indicate that they are alive, but the cell phone is dying. I'm going to venture a guess that since the phone has never been used, it probably hasn't been charged."

"Those factory charges don't last long," replied Michael.

"You're right, they don't. However, it is the noise at the end of the message that is of most concern."

"Oh, that loud 'pop' noise I heard?"

"Yes. Do you have any guesses as to what it might be?"

"I just thought it was the bad connection that we had."

"Well, for your information, that noise was identified by the computer as a handgun being discharged."

"You mean, somebody was shot on that airplane?"

"Yes. Now, are you ready to take on this mission?"

"You mean, extract them out of that country?"

"Yes."

"When do you want me to leave?"

"Whenever you're ready. Pack up whatever equipment you think you might need and then call the number on this card. A special detail will escort you to the airport," he said, handing Michael a business card with a solitary number engraved upon its face.

"Thank you and who do I have to talk to about my supplies list?"

"You can call my secretary and give her the list. I will make sure that you have everything before you leave the country."

"I'll start packing."

"Good luck."

Michael waited for the Director to leave before he started packing his own things. He called the Director's secretary and gave her a list of items he thought he was going to need on this mission. She wrote down everything and passed it along to the Director.

Michael finished packing up and put his stuff outside his apartment door. He called the number on the card and a car came and picked him up. He asked the driver to make one stop on the way to the airport, but the driver refused.

"Why can't you stop at the office; I need my weapons," said Michael.

"You're weapons of choice are already aboard the plane, sir."

"Oh, how thoughtful of the Director."

"He is a very smart man and has thought of everything."

"Oh, joy, this is going to be fun."

Michael put his head back against the headrest in the car and then exited the car when it came to a stop in front of the charter jet hangar. Michael stepped out of the car and walked up the ramp of a chartered Boeing 757-400C series airplane. As soon as Michael and his gear were aboard, the flight attendant closed the door and the pilot started the engines. Soon, the plane was taxiing and in a few minutes, the plane was lifting off the ground into the air.

The landing gear banged aboard. As the plane slowly banked to the southeast, Michael couldn't help but wonder who had been shot. He tried not to think about the matter any further and closed his eyes. Soon he was asleep for the rest of the flight.

The next time he opened his eyes, he rolled over in the seat he was in and stretched a little bit. He then rubbed his eyes and looked out the window to see nothing but water below him. He then looked around and saw that the flight attendant was bringing him something to drink.

"Excuse me, but, where are we?" asked Michael, as he sipped the coffee that had been brought him.

"We are over the Atlantic Ocean, en route to Rota, Spain. We should be landing there in a few hours to refuel."

"Thank you."

Michael went back to sipping his coffee and waited for the plane to land. Once the plane had stopped moving, Michael made his way to the flight deck. He knocked on the door. The navigator opened the door and Michael poked his head inside. The instrument panels were completely digitalized and very easy to read.

"Can I ask the pilot a question?" asked Michael to the navigator.

"What can I do for you, Mr. Pigeon?" asked the pilot.

"This plane is very similar to the 767 isn't it?"

"Yes, in many respects. The 767 is a little bit bigger than the 757, but the 767 operates just like the 737. The 767 has a longer flight duration than the 737."

"What's the minimum amount of airspeed needed for take off?"

"Minimum takeoff speed for the 767 is 250 kilometers an hour."

"What's the minimum runway distance?"

"About 1 kilometer of runway. However, you could get airborne quicker by doing the following."

The pilot showed Michael what to do to get the airplane in the air quicker. Michael took mental notes on what to do as he returned to his seat. In a matter of hours, he was in a foreign country being met by former Spetsnatz personnel who took him and his gear way out into the desert to their campsite. Michael was thankful that they were friendly and that they were prepared for his arrival. He took one last look around him the next morning before meeting with the colonel who was in charge.

CHAPTER 4

▼

Secretary of State Everett was lying facedown in the medical ward of the plane. Bill and the other diplomats were checking on her and providing her water and any food that was brought to them. Having resisted an attempt to sexually assault her, she was punished by being shot in the back with a 9mm pistol. The bullet however, was still inside her.

Bill was talking with the other diplomats about the situation, with Everett present. As Bill was changing her bandages, he looked down at her and then up at the other diplomats. They were all huddled around the medical ward's entryway.

"Only a coward shoots someone in the back!" yelled Bill to himself.

"I wonder why no one has sent troops in to get us out yet?" asked Bill.

"That is a little odd, isn't it?" replied the one diplomat.

"I wonder if my cell phone call got through to Michael," said Everett, her speech slurring a little.

"You need some rest, madam Secretary," replied the other diplomat.

"I would think that Michael is doing something about it right now. What about the UN?" asked Bill of the diplomats.

"I would have thought that, after we did not report to the next country on our list, someone would have started asking questions. What about that super secret UN extraction force you have, Mr. Ambassador?" asked the one diplomat to the one sitting to this left.

"I would have thought they would have determined where we are and sent them already. What about you, Mr. Ambassador?" he said, pointing towards the diplomat on his right.

"I'm surprised that anyone knows about the UN extraction forces. They are all volunteers, you know, and they carry no identification with them."

"Gentlemen, lets stop arguing right now; its not going to get us anywhere. They killed the pilots, so they are reasonably certain that no one can fly the plane. The plane's emergency locator beacon is laying in pieces on the hangar floor. Our satellite and other communications are trashed as well," said Bill.

"I see what you mean, sir. However, I do have an idea and I want to check on it. If you will excuse me." The diplomat stood up and went forward into the cockpit.

While everyone was trying to figure out a way to communicate to the outside world, the diplomat was turning on switches. He found that the plane was still almost fully fueled and the planes' transponder beacons were still functional. He turned the switches off and exited the cockpit just as the morning patrol was coming into the hangar to let them bathe and go to the bathroom. The diplomat came back and had a big smile on his face as he looked at Bill. Bill looked back at him but said nothing.

After the hostages were taken to be bathed and go to the bathroom, they were returned to the plane. Bill looked down at Everett who was still breathing, but in need of surgery to remove the bullet and repair the damage. He offered her some water and some food. After taking in the food and water, she turned her face upward to look Bill in the face.

"I saw the one diplomat from Neltoria going forward to the cockpit, what was he doing?" she asked.

"I don't know. He walked passed me and smiled, but didn't say anything."

"I hope Michael can save us, because I don't trust the UN to do it even though they have an elite extraction force for such occasions," she said, coughing a little.

"Rest now, madam Secretary."

Meanwhile, Michael was sitting in the tent of the former Spetsnatz unit that was very close to the border with the country of Lenora.

The colonel of the unit and Michael were talking. Since Michael could speak Russian, they were able to converse much easier. The colonel was happy to speak with Michael since he had heard so much about him from his brother.

Michael found out that the colonel's brother was the captain of the nuclear attack submarine that had rescued him a few years earlier. Michael and the colonel were discussing plans on how to determine which one of the airstrips was where they were being held. Speaking in Russian, they conversed.

"Mr. Pigeon, what is your plan right now?" asked the colonel.

"Right now, I need to have reconnaissance work done. I need to find out what goes on at those airstrips."

"I will send my men in there to observe what is going on. Is there anything else?"

"Do you have desert camouflage netting and do you have a sniper rifle?"

"I do have desert camouflage and, yes, I do have a sniper rifle."

"Does the sniper rifle come with at least a 30-round magazine?"

"Yes, I have 30-round magazines for the rifle."

"How much ammunition do you have for the rifle?"

"I currently have 75,000 rounds of 7.62mm X 54R."

"Good. I will expect a report on the reconnaissance reporting in the next few days."

"You will get it, Mr. Pigeon."

Meanwhile, in Washington D.C., the President of the United States called the State Department. Secretary Everett's secretary answered the phone. The woman seemed pleasant enough as she spoke to the President.

"Good morning, Mr. President, what can I do for you, sir?" she asked.

"A good morning to you, too. Is the Assistant Secretary of State in yet?" he asked.

"Yes, sir, he just arrived a few minutes ago."

"Can I speak with him?"

"One moment, sir."

There was silence on the line before it started ringing. The phone kept ringing until it was answered. The Assistant Secretary of State had just completed a business meeting in his office and smiled as he answered the phone.

"Good morning, Mr. President, what can I do for you?" asked Assistant Secretary of State Tyrone Franks.

"I'll make this short and sweet. Get over to my office in 20 minutes and come in through the Treasury Department building. I'll see you soon, goodbye."

The President hung up the phone. Tyrone hung up his phone and had his secretary reschedule all the morning appointments. As he walked out the door of the State Department building, he flagged down a taxicab. He arrived at the front doors of the Treasury Department building and walked into the lobby area. There he stood in front of the security officer's desk. She stood up and recognized Tyrone.

"Assistant Secretary of State Franks, can I help you with something?" she asked.

"Yes, I have my identification here, but how the hell do you get to the White House from here?!" he said, almost panicked, as he fumbled with his identification.

"I'll take care of it, please stand over there by the pillars and an escort will arrive shortly."

"Thank you, Cindy," he said, looking at her nametag.

The Assistant Secretary of State was escorted though the maze under the Treasury Department building to the White House. He stepped out of the elevator and walked into the Oval Office without going through the front door. As the President spun around in his chair, Tyrone noticed that there were other high-ranking officials in the room. Tyrone cleared his throat.

"Mr. President, what's going on?" asked Tyrone.

"Please have a seat. Do you know who these other people are?" asked the President.

"Yes, sir. They are, from right to left, the Director of the Central Intelligence Agency, Roger Smith. The Chief Intelligence Officer, Jonathan Greer for the CIA and the Chief of Counter-Terrorism Nate Kozee."

"Very good. Now, effective right this minute, by my Executive authority, you are to assume the full duties of the Office of the Secretary of State. You will continue to serve in this position as the Secretary of State until further notice or properly relieved by Executive authority."

"Jesus Christ, what the hell is going on?" asked Tyrone, now very concerned.

"We have a situation that has gone out of control. I have a packet here that will explain all of the particulars, as we know them. For right now, if anyone asks, like the press, the Secretary of State is recovering from her long trip at the military hospital outside of Washington, D.C. She suffered a food poisoning attack at a dinner last night, but is expected to make a full recovery," said the President.

"Food poisoning? Oh, God, I'm not ready for this," said Tyrone as he left the same way he came.

"Have a nice day, Mr. Secretary of State," said the Director of the CIA.

An hour later, he was walking into the outer office of the Secretary of State. Her secretary looked up at him and smiled.

"Frank, are you alright?" she asked.

"Not exactly, but, yes, if anyone asks. As of now, I am the Secretary of State until properly relieved by Executive authority of the President of United States."

"Good. Then you are scheduled to have lunch with the Secretary of Defense in half an hour. What's wrong with Miss Everett?" she asked.

"For your information and if anybody else asks, a food poisoning attack at a dinner last night. She is expected to make a full recovery at the military hospital outside of Washington, D.C."

"Food poisoning? Okay," said the secretary, rolling her eyes as Tyrone walked passed her into the office and shut the door.

Once inside, he tore open the envelope and read the contents. Afterwards, he tossed the contents and the envelope into the shredder. Sitting back down at his desk, he tried to calm himself down.

Meanwhile, Secretary Everett wasn't doing well. Even though the hostage takers had supplied Bill with a first aid kit to treat gunshot wounds, Bill and the other two diplomats knew that time was running out. After Everett had dozed off, Bill walked out of the room with the other diplomat. Bill made sure that the door was closed and locked. They walked to the rear of the aircraft before speaking.

"She's not doing well, is she?" asked the one diplomat from the Greater Antilles Islands.

"No, she is dying. That bullet wound, although it has started to heal, is going to cause her to go into shock here shortly from loss of blood," replied Bill.

"I wish we could do more."

"Well, so do I, however, they have abided by UN regulations in the treatment of hostages or prisoners or whatever we are considered by them."

"I'm about to lose hope, Bill. Will her death be painful?"

"Yes and no. Yes it will be, but no it doesn't have to be."

"I hope your country is sending your entire military force to wipe these imbeciles off the planet."

"You can count on it," replied Bill as he looked towards the forward door.

Meanwhile, Michael was going over the reports from the nightly reconnaissance missions. The men were tired when they returned from their trip, but nothing out of the ordinary could be seen in the reports. Michael then asked the men to take pictures as well as taking notes. So, for the next several nights the men gathered more information and pictures. This turned out to be a little more fruitful.

On the third night, Michael noticed something peculiar about one of the airstrips. There was an entire squadron of fighter jets and several surface-to-air missile batteries around the place.

Michael also noticed that the infrared pictures taken showed multiple heat sources. Michael decided on a bold move. That night, Michael was going with the reconnaissance unit to the middle airstrip.

"Colonel, I'm going to go with your men to the second airstrip tonight," said Michael in Russian.

"Did you find something interesting?"

"I think so, colonel. I find it very unusual that an airstrip would have a whole fighter squadron on the ground and no one walking around guarding any of it."

"Good luck tonight."

Michael went to his tent and went to sleep. When nightfall approached, the captain of the reconnaissance unit awakened him. Michael dressed into some black clothing that had been provided to him. Off they all went across the border in a vehicle that had a large piece of canvas draped over it.

Inside, the canvas was supported by many small pieces of metal forming a framework. From the outside, the canvas had been painted to look like a rhinoceros. Anyone looking at the vehicle would think it was a rhinoceros as well.

In the dead of the night, driving slowly so as to not attract unnecessary attention, the vehicle headed towards the point where the captain had been conducting his observations. After parking the vehicle and crawling out from under the canvas, Michael and the men all laid down on a sand dune not far from the end of the airstrip. Michael looked at the whole scene before surveying the entire piece of property with both binoculars and the infrared equipment.

Michael watched for a few hours and noted that no one was guarding the planes. He saw the surface-to-air missile batteries all along the runway. He then looked at the one and only hangar next to the tower. He looked into the tower and saw people sitting at their radar stations. He then looked at the top of the tower to see the turning radar assembly. He looked around some more before looking around the airfield itself.

The fighter jets were parked all in neat rows facing inwards at each other. They all looked like they could be manned and ready at a moments notice. That's when Michael noticed something about the airstrip that gave it all away. Michael scanned the entire airfield from one end to the other. That's when Michael decided that this might be the airfield where Bill, Everett and the others were being held hostage.

Michael put the binoculars down and then yawned. Everyone piled back into the vehicle and were safely transported back to the campsite. After stepping out of the vehicle, Michael rubbed his eyes and walked into the tent with the communications gear. The man looked up at Michael. Speaking Russian, they conversed.

"Can you get in touch with the CIA? I need to have Jonathan Greer do something for me," asked Michael.

"Yes, sir. Tell me what you need done and I will transmit it."

"Tell Jonathan Greer that I would like ground penetrating radar pictures of the second airfield. Please give him the GPS coordinates of the airfield."

"Yes, sir."

The man was transmitting Michael's request as Michael departed the communications tent. On the way to the armory, Michael stopped by the colonel's tent. He looked up as Michael walked inside, closing the door behind himself. Speaking Russian, they conversed.

"Good to see you, Mr. Pigeon. My communications man just told me that you asked for some unusual pictures," said the colonel.

"Yes, I did. A hunch I have. By the way, I will need the sniper rifle tonight with armor piercing rounds and a silencer. How soon could Lenora mount an attack after being alerted to a possible invasion?" asked Michael.

"I have estimated three hours for a full ground assault. However, they can launch an air attack in just a few minutes. You may pick up the rifle when you leave my tent."

"Thank you, colonel. Now, I have a big favor to ask of you."

"What favor can I do for you?"

"If I prove my theory correct tonight, please provide me with a distraction when the time comes."

"Did you have anything in particular in mind?"

"Lots of noise and create the maximum amount of confusion possible."

"I will do my best."

While Michael was asleep that day, Everett slipped into a coma. Following the instructions posted on the life support system in the plane's medical room, Bill and the other diplomat that had some advance medical training from being in his country's military, hooked her up to the machine. Bill looked at the instructions on the battery power pack. He then looked at the diplomat as the machine hissed to life.

"We have four battery power packs. They will last her four days. After that, those batteries are dead and so is she," said Bill.

"Is it time to give up, Bill?"

"No, not yet. If I know Michael Pigeon, he will use all of his resources to find us."

"I certainly hope so, Bill," the diplomat said, as he left the room.

"Michael, I hope you can hear this prayer for all of us, including Everett."

Meanwhile, Michael had set himself up to shoot at the people in the tower. As he loaded up the rifle, the captain looked at Michael with some grave concern on his face. The captain wasn't sure that the whole thing wasn't some sort of last-ditch effort. The captain spoke to Michael in Russian.

"Mr. Pigeon, I don't understand what is going on, could you please explain it to me?" asked the captain.

"Captain, during World War two, we would sometimes set up decoy airfields and airplanes. The enemy would see these decoys and bomb them not realizing that they were nothing more than cardboard or plywood painted up to look like the real thing," said Michael, as he looked through the scope.

"And you think this airfield is a decoy, as you call it?"

"I'll find out in a minute and if the ground penetrating radar pictures I asked for come in like I think they will, this is the place where they're being held. Now, if you will excuse me, I have to shoot here," he replied, checking to make sure the silencer was properly attached to the rifle.

"I am sorry, sir."

Michael set his sights on the bricks just below where the person was sitting watching their radar screen. He racked the action back on the rifle and let the bolt close on the first round of the magazine. Michael fired a round off and it impacted the brick. While Michael watched for the round to ricochet and hear the report of such, no noise came back to his ears.

He looked through his scope and found that the person was still sitting upright. Michael fired off rounds at the planes and the other buildings until the magazine was empty. He then gave the rifle back to the captain and used the binoculars.

There, on the "brick" of the tower was a neat bullet hole. As Michael looked closer at the tower "people", he found bullet holes in them but no blood. They were still standing or sitting at their stations. They didn't seem to be breathing. That's when Michael realized that this was a decoy airstrip. He put the binoculars back up and looked at the captain.

"Dummies, captain. Mannequins, fake people with real uniforms on them," said Michael.

"Lenora has a very clever person to have thought of putting uniforms on dummies."

"Which means all of this out here is a fake with the exception of the hangar. It seems pretty solid. Come on, let's go back to camp and we will discuss further plans."

They all drove back to the campsite. As Michael stepped out of the vehicle, the communications person approached him. He shoved a stack of pictures into Michael's left hand and departed.

Michael looked at the photos and noticed that there were no fuel tanks under the tarmac. The whole airstrip was a fake. Nodding his head, he tossed the pictures into a trashcan and walked into the colonel's tent. Speaking Russian, they conversed.

"Colonel, tell the CIA that I have found them. I will affect a rescue tomorrow morning. I need that distraction."

"How are you going to get across the border?"

"Using your vehicle."

"Is there anything else you need for this mission?"

"I'll need some of that desert camouflage netting that I asked for earlier."

"Yes, sir," replied the colonel, as he picked up the phone on his desk.

CHAPTER 5

▼

Under the cover of desert camouflage netting, Michael started the slow and arduous task of penetrating the border without being seen. Michael had taken with him several days worth of food and water. In addition to these supplies, he told both the colonel and the captain where he would be staying at near the airfield.

As the heat of the day wore on, Michael slept under the netting and, at night, he would move about with some ease. More than once, a patrol had come by very near to him. In fact, one patrol had come close enough for Michael to see them. He was prepared to take them out if necessary.

Meanwhile, news had reached the Central Intelligence Agency about Michael's finding. The Director of the CIA called an emergency meeting with both the President and some key military personnel. As everyone gathered in the small room at Langley, Virginia, Jonathan Greer was just receiving the last page of the translated intelligence report. He grabbed it and ran to the meeting room, reading it along the way. Jonathan Greer entered the room and went to the front to stand behind the podium.

"I have just received word that Michael has possibly located the hostages," started Jonathan Greer.

"Are we sure it is them?" asked the President.

"We have no concrete proof that is them, but the observations from Michael would seem to indicate such is the case," replied the Director of the CIA.

"What observations are those?" asked General Delmonte of the U.S. Air Force.

"Michael encountered an entire airstrip full of planes that were nothing more than plywood. He then shot at the tower and discovered that the tower wasn't made of brick, but of plywood and possibly foam rubber. He also observed that ground penetrating radar pictures showed no fuel tanks under the tarmac to refuel planes with, sir," said the intelligence chief.

"What about the hangar?" asked General Delmonte.

"The hangar is very real, but our satellite shots are being blocked by some sort of shielding material."

"What is the condition of the Secretary of State and the others?" asked the President.

"Unknown at this time, sir."

"Do we have any information on their air defenses?" asked General Delmonte.

"Yes and no. Yes we have some, but no we cannot confirm or deny this information."

"I'll be the judge of that, chief. Tell me what we know and who supplied this information," he said, pulling out a pen from his military uniform's upper left pocket and pad of paper from the upper right pocket.

"The information comes from Colonel Godinov's reconnaissance teams."

"Did you say Colonel Godinov?"

"Yes."

"Gentlemen, I will wager that the information is more than likely very accurate. The good Colonel Godinov is former Spetsnatz," replied General Delmonte.

"Former Soviet Special Forces?" asked the President.

"Yes, sir. Tell me what information you have, chief."

"They have a total of 10 airfields. All of them loaded with attack helicopters of Soviet design and some old F-4 Phantoms and Mig-29's. They appear to have a very quick air defense response time, but their ground troops are hours away from anything in the country."

"What is the colonel's estimated air response time?"

"About three to five minutes, General Delmonte."

"And we still don't know about the condition of the party aboard."

"That's correct, general. Now, as I was saying, Michael Pigeon is moving across the border sometime tonight, our time, to try and affect a rescue or fly the plane out of their airspace."

"Those people could blast that civilian jetliner right out of the sky with those Mig-29's. What about surface-to-air missile batteries?"

"They have somewhere between 60 to 100 of them scattered throughout the country."

"We need a plan and quick. General Delmonte, assuming that the plane is able to fly, where is the nearest friendly airspace and airport?" asked the President.

"The nearest friendly airspace is 80 nautical miles to the east. But, that plane would take some time to cover that distance. By then, that country would blast them out of the sky."

"We still need a plan, general. One that is flexible and able to be deployed immediately."

"I hear you, Mr. President. But, until I know the condition of the hostages, I won't commit to anything."

"I understand, general. Please be on your way."

"Yes, sir."

When the general had left, the President turned to face the intelligence chief and the Director at the same time. He looked sternly at both before speaking.

"I don't want this administration to hand over those hostages to any foreign power that deals in hostage taking or terrorism. I also want an open channel kept at all times for when Michael Pigeon communicates," said the President.

"Yes, sir, I can arrange for the open communications line. What next?" asked the Director.

"When we have confirmation of the condition of the hostages, we need to move into action. Chief, please keep me informed of any developments."

"Yes, sir."

"Now, not a word of this leaves here. As far as anyone knows, the Secretary of State is recovering from food poisoning at the military hospital near here."

"I understand, sir."

The President left the building and the Director and the Chief were standing there. Both of them went to their respective departments, while, half a world away, Michael was waking up from his nap when a patrol started setting up camp right next to his. Michael waited silently, sweating profusely in the late afternoon sun.

More than once he thought he might have to give himself away by shaking off the sweat that had run down his forehead to the edges of his eyebrows and the tip of his nose. Instead, he let it drip off so he wouldn't move. As the heat of the day drove most of the patrol into their own tents, Michael waited until they were all eating dinner before breaking his camp.

Silently, Michael slipped out of his campsite and carefully took his supplies with him over the sand dune to the bottom of the dune. He then crawled back up the sand dune to get his netting. He looked around and grabbed the netting, disappearing in the blink of an eye. Michael climbed out of the sand dune and into another one, checking periodically for anyone who might be following him. Since no one followed him, he moved through the desert night with ease towards the airfield.

Just as the Russian reconnaissance patrol was returning to their side of the border, they met up with Michael. They quickly took Michael's exhausted food and empty water bottles and exchanged them for fresh ones. Michael set up camp right around daybreak. He set up his booby traps around his campsite and then spread out a thin blanket so he could sleep on the still cool ground.

With the sun reaching its zenith around noon, Michael stayed asleep until he heard the whine of a diesel engine approaching. He woke up, rubbed his eyes and yawned almost choking at the site that greeted him.

There, less than 10 meters away was a military vehicle. Michael held his breath as the men exited the vehicle and started setting up a mobile surface-to-air missile launcher. Michael kept a keen eye on them and their movements. They soon moved the radar dish out to the other side of Michael's campsite running the lines right straight over his netting.

When the men were finished with setting up the battery, one

of them walked right over to where Michael was sleeping. The man proceeded to urinate less than one meter from Michael. When the man was done, Michael waited until he was gone before breathing a heavy sigh of relief.

Meanwhile, inside the hangar, another battery power pack had been changed. For Everett, this was her only way to stay alive. As Bill closed the door to the medical area, he tossed the used up battery onto one of the seats. He sat down and put his head into his cupped hands.

He closed his eyes and said a prayer for Everett. Both Bill and the others knew that the battery pack that was in there was the last one. Once it quit working, the machine would shut itself off, suffocating Everett. Bill looked up to see one of the diplomats standing in front of him.

"I just put in the last battery power pack," said Bill.

"You did your best, now, it is up to our respective governments to come up with a plan," the diplomat replied, putting his hands on Bill's shoulders.

"When the battery power pack dies, so she does of suffocation," said Bill, trying not to cry.

Meanwhile, Michael was trying to figure out how to get into the hangar without setting off any alarms, if there were any alarms. Michael came out that night and looked over the place. There were now several patrols of real men walking the perimeter and manning up more anti-aircraft batteries. Michael knew this wasn't going to be easy, but he was going to get inside that hangar at all costs. He started formulating a plan that would work if only he could figure out how to get onto the tarmac and not be noticed. He decided to take out the outpost sentry.

Meanwhile, General Delmonte, after having looked over all his options, couldn't come up with one. Retiring for the evening, he went home only to find that he could not sleep. He made himself a drink and sat down to listen to the morning news report. Finally, his mind was starting to calm down when the thought hit him.

He slammed the drink down, showered, shaved and took the mass transit system into his office. Since it was Sunday, not many people would notice his coming or going. He entered the Pentagon Building at a brisk pace.

He opened up his office and turned on the lights. As he looked at the maps of air force bases, he was looking for the closest friendly one to where Michael was located. General Delmonte located a base in Egypt.

He quickly pulled up the file on the air base and found out it was used for training B-2 Stealth and F-117 Stealth Fighter pilots. The aircrews were all female and all qualified in basic air defense penetration. He located their phone number and called the base via a secure phone.

"Good afternoon, El-Alamein Air Operations Base, 7119ᵗʰ Air Defense Squadron, Captain Dickey speaking, how may I help you?" she said.

"A good afternoon to you, Captain Dickey. This is General Delmonte, is your commanding officer available?"

"Yes, sir, one moment," she said as she put the general on hold.

A short time later, Colonel Roberta Minetz came on the line.

"General Delmonte, what can I do for you, sir?" she said, trying to get her flight uniform on while talking on the phone.

"How many planes do you have?"

"Is this a secure line, sir?"

"Yes."

"We have 10 B-2, Stealth Bombers and 12 F-117, Stealth Fighters."

"Do you have ordinance there?"

"Yes, sir. I have all types."

"Are your aircrews current on their air defense system penetration training?"

"Yes, sir. What he hell is going on, sir?"

"You will be receiving instructions from me within the hour. Follow those instructions precisely, General Minetz."

"Yes, sir."

Colonel Minetz hung up the phone. She turned around to face her executive officer, Lieutenant Colonel Charlene Lowestein. Lowestein looked at her commanding officer uneasily.

"Executive officer, please alert me the minute General Delmonte's orders arrive, that is all," she said as she left the commanding officer's building.

Meanwhile, as luck would have it, some of the men were opening the hangar doors up. As the doors were opened, the lights inside were changed to red instead of the normal white. Michael crept along the fence trying to get a glimpse of what was inside. He rounded a bend and almost ran straight into a patrol. He lowered himself to the ground slowly so that no one would see what was going on.

As he approached a gate on the north side of the airfield, he heard a large truck driving up the road towards the gate. The passenger jumped out and opened the gate up. As he was getting back into the truck, Michael jumped into the back of the open bay to discover food and medical supplies were being delivered.

Once the truck was inside the airfield, Michael jumped out of the back when the truck slowed down to go inside the hangar. Michael rolled onto the tarmac and under one of the planes that Michael had seen earlier. He reached out and touched the underside of the plane and found out it was made out of plywood. He stood up when the last patrol went by and walked slowly up behind them.

When the patrol walked into the guard shack next to the hangar, they started to close the hangar doors. Michael waited until the guard had turned his back and then darted into the hangar and quickly spotted some fuel drums where he could hide for the evening. Michael looked behind himself as the hangar door finished closing and the locks were engaged.

Michael waited until the last patrol had finished checking the fuel drums and had taken out the trash before making his move. Conveniently, those same persons shut off the lights in the hangar allowing Michael to move around more freely. Michael waited until the guards were back in the shack before running quickly across the hangar to the front landing gear. He looked around and saw one of the guards looking his direction. The guard came out and said something to his friend. Michael listened in as best he could.

"I thought I saw movement out there in the hangar next to the landing gear," the man said pulling out his 9mm semi-automatic pistol and racking the action on it.

"Relax, there's no one else out here but our patrol unit. Maybe you saw a big, ugly RAT!" he yelled.

"Yeah, maybe," the man replied, putting the pistol back into the holster.

Michael had seen the look on the man's face. The man was scared to death of rats. Michael filed this away in the back of his mind for future use. He watched the guards go back to disassembling their rifles, cleaning them and putting them back together. Michael climbed up inside the forward landing gear storage area and opened the maintenance hatch into the cargo hold.

Once he was inside the cargo hold, he closed the hatch quietly. He started walking towards the rear of the aircraft. He was looking for the maintenance ladder from the cargo hold into the cockpit. It was dark and several times he ran into things. This caused him to have to walk slower and feel more in front of him before stepping in that direction. Finally, his right hand touched a ladder.

The ladder, Michael surmised, led up into the cockpit. Cautiously, he climbed up the ladder and then opened the hatch, slowly at first, to about a quarter of an inch. He listened intently for any sounds of movement. When he had listened for several minutes and heard nothing, he threw the hatch completely open. Quickly he exited the cargo hold.

The cockpit was deserted so Michael closed the hatch and noticed that there was a little bit of light coming in from the few lights left on in the hangar. He looked out the cockpit door peephole and saw no guards or anyone else inside the immediate area so he opened it slowly.

Looking both ways, he opened the door and then closed it as quietly as he could. After the latch had clicked into place, Michael looked around to see the galley to his left and the closed forward door to his right. He thought he heard someone coming, so he ducked into the galley.

He saw that it was Bill, who didn't see Michael standing just a few centimeters from him. As Bill turned around, he saw Michael standing there and almost choked. Gasping for breath, he grabbed Michael by the shoulders and shook him.

"Hello, Bill, sorry it took so long, but I had problems finding you," said Michael.

"I'm glad you're here. I'll expect a full report when we get out of this mess," said Bill.

"Will do. How is everyone?"

"Not good. A few days ago, they tried to sexually assault Everett. She resisted and one of those guards shot her in the back."

"How bad is she?"

"Take a look for yourself."

Michael followed Bill back to the medical room. When Michael opened the door, he saw her on the life support machine. He closed the door and almost gagged. He turned to look at Bill.

"She doesn't look good, Bill."

"And, unfortunately, I installed the last battery power pack this morning. She has less than 24-hours to live."

"Why?"

"That life support machine will quit working in that time because it needs these battery power packs to function. When the battery power pack dies, the machine shuts off and she suffocates."

"I'll do what I can, Bill."

"Here, take this with you," Bill said, handing Michael one of the spent battery power packs.

"I'll be back tonight."

"I'll see you then."

Michael took the heavy battery power pack and left the plane. He had to wait until the next morning when the food and other supplies arrived to duck out the side of the hangar door. He then had to hide in the shadows until he could make it to his campsite.

When he arrived at his campsite, he noticed that the anti-aircraft battery had been moved and was no longer a threat to him. As he entered his netting, the captain of the reconnaissance squad met him. Speaking Russian, they conversed.

"Good to see you, captain. Would you please give this to your supply officer and tell him I need at least two of them tonight?" said Michael, handing over the battery power pack.

"I will let him know. We left you fresh supplies after they repositioned the anti-aircraft missile battery. Did you make contact with the hostages?"

"Yes. They are all right with the exception of Everett; she is in critical condition with a gunshot wound to the back. She is on life support."

"I will let the colonel know. Is there anything else I can obtain for you?"

"Yes, a remote controlled, ugly rat."

"Yes, sir. Good luck."

Michael was left alone to think and try to get some sleep. The heat of the day was beginning to make things worse. Michael could only hope that the deception of the rhino could not be easily seen through. As Michael lay down on the blanket on the still cool earth, his dreams were filled with the images of Everett suffocating when the machine stopped working.

CHAPTER 6

▼

Meanwhile, in Washington, D.C., General Delmonte, was putting the final touches on his plans. He finished them off and filed them away on his laptop, turning it off. He reached across the desk and dialed the White House.

He set himself up an appointment and since the appointment was in just a few minutes, he left his office. Once he had arrived at the White House, he saw the President without delay. After the general was satisfied that no one was going to walk in on them, he revealed his plans to the President.

"Mr. President, I have put the 7119th Air Defense Squadron on alert to receive these orders and to follow them without question," said General Delmonte.

"I think that this plan of yours is very commendable. If everyone makes it through this in one piece, I intended on giving everyone a medal of some kind."

"I'm sure that will be greatly appreciated, Sir. However, I need to get this out this afternoon on the priority message traffic. If you will excuse me, Sir."

"By all means, thank you for stopping by," said the President as the general exited the Oval Office.

Meanwhile, the supply officer was gathering up the requested items that Michael had requested. The battery power packs, he could only get two and stuffed them into the bag that was going to be used to shuttle the equipment to Michael. As the supply officer stuffed the remote controlled, ugly, hairy rat into the bag, which he had a hard time finding in the first place, he wondered what Michael was going to use it for.

He closed up the bag and handed it to the commanding officer who inspected the items. He handed the bag back so that the items could be delivered to Michael. Before he left the commanding officer's tent, he turned to face the colonel.

"Comrade colonel, what does Michael need with a remote control rat?" asked the supply officer.

"I don't know, but I was told that he is very creative when it comes to getting in and out of places. He must have some need for this item or he wouldn't have asked for it. Now, make sure that it gets to him tonight and tell him that I sent the message off already."

"Yes, comrade colonel."

Meanwhile, in Langley, Virginia, Jonathan looked over the message that had been received and was gravely concerned. He put the message down and called the Director at home.

"Yes, John, what can I do for you?" asked Roger.

"I have a message from Michael. He has found them alive."

"That is excellent, is your operative cooperating with Michael liked I asked?"

"Yes, sir. However, there may be some complications with the rescue attempt."

"What kind of problems?"

"The report states that the Secretary of State is gravely wounded. A gunshot wound to the back. She is on the plane's life support system."

"Oh, shit, that little problem is going to drastically complicate any efforts at extraction."

"Yes, sir, you're right. I would like to apologize for dragging you out of bed at this hour."

"No, don't worry about calling me at this hour, it's not a problem. Where is the nearest medical facility that we can get the Secretary of State to once she is out of that country?"

"I don't know, sir. I would guess that either Rota, Spain or Naples, Italy would be within the range of that plane."

"You're not seriously considering that Michael is going to fly that plane out of the country? He would be a dead duck the minute he got airborne."

"Sir, if Secretary Everett is that gravely injured, the plane may be the only way out of that country."

"How far to the nearest medical facility by road?"

"Several days at best, at worst, several weeks. She won't last that long."

"Okay, I hear you. Tell Michael to use the plane, if he can. If not, he is to come up with a suitable alternative to get everyone out of there."

"Yes, sir, I will send that message along."

"Good night, John."

"Good night, sir."

Roger hung up the phone and called the President immediately to inform him of the situation. The President was upset at the news that Secretary Everett had been shot in the back, but was thankful that she was still alive. When the President hung up the phone, he stepped out of bed and called General Delmonte to tell him of the news.

General Delmonte was really upset with the news because now the plans had to be changed. He decided to call Colonel Minetz directly to modify the orders. The general had the colonel woke up for the phone call.

"Colonel Minetz, this is General Delmonte. There has been an emergency modification to your orders," he started off saying.

"Yes, sir, I hear you. There has been an emergency modification to my original orders," she said, pulling up the orders that she had been handed a few hours earlier and pulling out a pen from her flight suit.

"Secretary of State Everett has been gravely wounded. She is on life support at this time. The plane is going to be the only way out of the country. Your squadron will have to fly interference for the plane. The plane is to be escorted safely to the nearest medical facility."

"Sir, would that be Rota, Spain or Naples, Italy?"

"Which one do you think the plane should go to?"

"According to my air charts, Rota, Spain is 330 nautical miles further than Naples, Italy, sir."

"Okay, then the plane is to proceed, escorted by your squadron, to Naples, Italy."

"Yes, sir."

"Please follow the rest of the orders about running interference in that air space and please be advised that I will call you when I have received word that the plane is airborne."

"Yes, sir."

"As of right now, your squadron is on full alert. Fully fuel your planes and fully arm them as per the orders I sent you."

"Yes, sir."

"Good afternoon, colonel."

The general hung up the phone. When Colonel Minetz had hung up her phone, she called the airbase tower and put them on full alert from this time frame forward per General Delmonte's orders. The females all rolled out of their barracks and drove out to the planes on the tarmac in the blazing sun. When they were all aboard their planes, fuel trucks showed up and started fueling each plane. When the fueling of the planes was completed, the ordinance personnel started loading up their ordinance bays.

Colonel Minetz climbed aboard her B-2 Stealth Bomber and started up her engines. As the engines started warming up, she looked out of the window of the aircraft up to the tower and put on her headphones. She then switched frequencies to be able to speak to all the other planes. She took in a deep breath and then spoke.

"Attention, all planes, this is Colonel Minetz. Per General Delmonte's orders, we have been placed on full alert status. Our mission is to provide interference for any surface-to-air or even air-to-air activities. These activities will be done in such a manner that once we have penetrated the enemy's airspace, they won't know what hit them," she said.

"Colonel Minetz, who is the enemy?" asked Captain Killen.

"The country of Lenora is the enemy. Now, we have all trained for this type of mission and we will do it well. I want you to know this, those who have the special orders packet in the flight registers are the ones who will have to escort the plane carrying a gravely injured Secretary of State to Naples, Italy; good luck to us all."

Colonel Minetz switched frequencies back to the tower. She commenced her pre-flight checklist like the others were doing. When she was done with this action, she looked back up to the tower and switched frequencies.

"Tower, this is Red Bird One. Request permission to taxi," she asked.

"Permission granted. Fuel trucks will refuel those that are below half load," said the air tower officer.

"Thank you. Is the blue phone working?" she asked.

"Yes, ma'am it is. My staff and I will be waiting along with you for the call."

"Thank you."

She taxied her B-2 Stealth Bomber out onto the taxiway. Once she was at the end of the taxiway, she turned her plane onto the runway's threshold and stopped it. She turned the engines back to idle and then opened the canopy of her plane.

She stood up and looked behind her plane. Everyone was parked neatly in a perfect line behind her plane. As she buckled back up and closed the canopy, she calculated that the special envelope that she had talked about would be being opened just about now.

The rest of the pilots and copilots were completing their pre-flight checklists. The last fighter jet had just completed the last thing on the checklist; opening the flight register. As she opened the flight register, she saw an envelope inside. She opened the envelope up and read the instructions before putting the envelope back into the flight register. She immediately contacted Colonel Minetz and asked her to switch to another frequency so that they could talk.

"Colonel, why was I chosen for this escort duty? I mean, my proficiency in these things is at best acceptable whereas Major Leland is much better," Captain Shelly said.

"Yes, she is better on the range, however, you are far better than her when under fire situations. Remember when I sent you both to the simulator?"

"Yes, some of those situations were simply awful."

"Right. Major Leland, I don't think, has what it takes to stay composed while under fire. You have that capacity and have demonstrated it numerous times."

"Thank you, colonel."

"You're welcome. Now, switch back to the tower frequency and try to get some sleep while we wait."

"Yes, ma'am."

Meanwhile, the supplies were delivered to Michael. Lenoran troop strength had increased along with surface-to-air missile batteries. Michael noticed that, now, there were guards all over the tarmac. They were lightly armed and didn't seem to be all that concerned that someone was watching them.

He waited until the food truck came into the compound before hiding among the food containers. Once he was inside the hangar, he watched as the food truck was searched on the underside and then inside. One of the men searching the vehicle was very angry that he had to check the place for a rat.

When the man had completed his search of the food truck and found no rat, the food truck was unloaded by Bill and the others while the guards watched them carefully. Bill saw Michael and winked his right eye at him as Michael gave Bill the two battery power packs. Michael watched as the hangar doors were opened once again for the evening. Michael thought this might come in handy later on so he filed this intelligence away for future reference.

That night, Michael climbed up inside the plane once again. This time he met the diplomats and the others that were aboard. He took the spent battery power pack and talked to all of them briefly.

"What is the series of this plane?" asked Michael.

"Series 400ER," said one of the diplomats.

Michael thought about this for more than a moment. He went into the cockpit and found that the radio had been removed. All the other equipment was left intact. He turned on a few switches and saw that the plane was 90 percent fueled. He looked again at the empty place where the radio had been and cursed under his breath. Leaving the cockpit, he rejoined the others.

"They removed the radio. We have no way to communicate with anyone," said Michael.

"We found that out too, Michael," said Bill.

"How is Everett doing?"

"She's fading with each day we stay here," said one of the diplomats.

"Then tomorrow morning, we are going to takeoff from here," announced Michael.

"How?" asked Bill.

"This place may be crawling with guards, but at least one of the guards isn't terribly fond of rats.

"Michael, I don't see how this is going to help us," said one of the diplomats.

"I plan on releasing a few diversions so that everyone is confused. Does anyone know what type of engine is installed on this plane?" asked Michael.

"Pratt and Whitney JT9G Turbofans," said the one diplomat with some jet experience.

"Thank you, sir. Now, I have to get out of here before they close the doors and put the finishing touches on the escape plans," said Michael as he departed.

Once he was outside the gates, he looked around and saw that there were lots of vehicles, so he had to slow them up somehow. He headed to his hideout and when the captain of the reconnaissance unit arrived with his requested items he gave him another list of items and spoke to him in Russian.

"I need to find some way of jamming the hangar door open," said Michael.

"I will bring something that will do the job tonight when we come back. Do you want me to tell my commanding officer?" he asked.

"Yes, tell him to prepare to sacrifice the rhino you all have."

"Yes, sir, I will tell him."

Meanwhile, the squadron had been sitting on the ground for over 13 hours now. They were impatient and fatigued. The colonel couldn't figure out what went wrong. The orders from General Delmonte were specific that they were on full alert. They had to be ready to fly in minutes. The colonel decided to call it quits at this point and had the planes refueled and shutdown.

After this was completed, she called the air squadron into the flight briefing room and had everyone relax for the rest of the day. She had just started to get some good sleep when the air tower officer called her barracks. The air tower officer said he had received a phone call from Strategic Air Command in Southern Europe to be ready to go soon.

The colonel woke everyone up and the planes were remanned. Everyone was back in their respective cockpits and again they played the waiting game. The planes were not made ready until such time as they were actually going to become airborne. That call came in shortly after everyone had completed their respective pre-flight checklist. The air tower officer was half asleep when the blue phone rang on the ledge that was next to where he was dozing. He picked it up.

Meanwhile, Michael had booby-trapped the entire platoon's vehicles with white phosphorous grenades. The heavy wire, which was woven through the pins, served as the way to pull the pins out. As he finished setting the last booby trap with the grenade in the fuel tank just like all the others, he pulled the wire very, very hard.

Explosions soon started going off and chaos resulted. Michael slipped into the hangar and climbed up into the cockpit after dropping off the remote controlled rat on the floor and turning it on. After the rat was turned on, he let it go and controlled it up to the guard shack.

The guard inside saw the rat and started shooting at it wildly and screaming. This all added to the chaos as the other personnel were dealing with what they thought was a charging rhino. The liquid steel adhesive that Michael had poured into the tracks of the hangar doors had hardened to complete hardness and Michael watched from the cockpit as the other guard tried to close the doors and they wouldn't close.

Michael cranked the engines over and within a few minutes, had departed the hangar. First light was just barely visible on the horizon. The guard in the shack was accidentally shot by the other guard trying to kill the rat. As more and more explosions went off, Michael had pulled onto the taxiway and headed to the far end of the runway.

Calmly, he buckled himself into the pilot's seat and was soon joined by Bill. Michael looked over at Bill as Michael rolled the plane onto the runway. Now, Michael and Bill could see that what few troops weren't chasing after something, or putting out a fire, were taking up a position to block the plane's departure. Michael looked up and stepped very hard down on the brake pedal. As he did this, he reached up and turned on both sets of auxiliary turbines for the engines.

"Bill, buckle your seatbelt, this is going to be a real quick takeoff.

When that light on the control panel on your side turns from red to green let me know," said Michael.

"Okay, Michael," he said, looking down at the light.

Meanwhile, the 7119th Air Defense Squadron had penetrated the Lenoran air space and everyone went about their various parts of the plan. The one lonely F-117 Stealth Fighter headed down low and towards the airfield. As she passed over a sand dune, she could see some of the back up air support coming in to help.

She counted seven F-4 Phantoms and six Mig-29's. She suddenly pulled up and disappeared into a small cloudbank. She then called her colonel to let them know what was going on with the enemy's air defenses.

"Little birdie to Red Bird One, you have company coming your direction. Seven Phantoms and six Mig's," she said confidently.

"Little birdie, this is Red Bird One, we will welcome them with open arms," replied the colonel.

The Lenoran air defenses, thought to be impenetrable, were now under attack by phantoms of a sort. Despite their best efforts on the ground and in the air, the funny looking black planes were not showing up on radar, making the surface-to-air missiles useless. Their commander told them that under no circumstances was the plane at the airfield allowed to leave the ground nor Lenoran air space.

Little birdie started to descend rapidly and came across another sand dune to see the chaos at the airfield and the plane just sitting there. She watched as a small group of vehicles started rolling down the runway to stop the plane from taking off. She swung her plane around and flew across the runway and did something that the personnel in the open-air vehicles weren't expecting.

CHAPTER 7

▼

She flew over their position and activated the afterburner, which shattered the sound barrier just barely 30 meters above their heads. They were all affected by the move. This also caused the drivers to lose control and drive off the runway into the median strip in between.

As they all exited their vehicles and held their ears, they were all screaming. The only sound that seemed to drown out their screams and explosions were the engines on the airplane that were running up higher and higher in pitch. Inside the plane, the whole plane was starting to shake.

Bill looked down at the red light and at nothing else. Michael was looking at the turbine pressures and speeds. They were increasing but not as fast he would have liked. Bill looked over at Michael who was intently watching the digital readouts. As the numbers reached 70 percent, he looked over at Bill and spoke.

"Bill, tell all those diplomats it's going to be a rough trip. They need to fasten their seatbelts and put their heads back against their headrests," said Michael.

Bill made the announcement and had no sooner than completed the announcement when he saw Michael move his right hand towards the throttle controls. Michael put his right hand on the controls and waited, watching the numbers pass 85 percent. When the numbers reached 95 percent, Bill looked down the runway and then down at the red light. Suddenly, it turned green.

"Green!" yelled Bill.

Michael let off the brake and slammed the throttle controls to the maximum setting. The plane lurched forward. Then it picked up speed very quickly. Michael looked down at the speed readout.

Minimum takeoff speed had been achieved in less than 300 meters. He waited until they were almost on top of the wrecked vehicles before climbing into the air. He folded up the landing gear and turned the plane towards the north and freedom.

Meanwhile, on the ground, one of the surface-to-air missile batteries hadn't been damaged during the attack. The operator, although disoriented by the sonic boom that followed the tiny black aircraft, managed to pull himself up into the chair that faced the controls. He then turned on a few switches and watched his radar screen.

The aircraft carrying the hostages that his country was planning on using as a bargaining chip in future negotiations was leaving their airspace. He picked up a phone and pressed a key that connected him directly to the Lenoran Air Defense headquarters. The man didn't care if anyone could hear him or not, he had important information that he had to pass along. Speaking in Lenoran, he yelled into the receiver.

"I have been deafened by the sonic shockwave from one of those American UFO planes."

The receiver of the message wasn't thrilled with being yelled at, so he yelled at the air defense officer. The air defense officer thought about it a moment and then issued an order.

"Tell that man to shoot the plane down!" he yelled.

"Yes, sir. Lenoran station two, Lenoran station two. You are to shoot down that plane. It is not, I repeat, not to leave Lenoran airspace!" the operator yelled.

The man on the other end had some of his hearing start to return. He vaguely made out the orders that were being issued to him. As he looked out of his surface-to-air missile battery, he saw, on the horizon, a large cloud of dust.

Calmly, he reached over to the fire control switch cover and opened it up. Looking back down to his radar screen he locked onto the plane. He then reached over and pushed the button and said something to himself out loud, not caring if anyone had heard him.

"I can't see you, my UFO planes, but I can see the other plane. I will blow you out of the sky," he said, as he pushed the button.

In an instant, all six surface-to-air missiles took to the air. Once they were airborne, they switched over to their frequency with radar feed from the site on the ground. The radar operator turned the set over to the missiles and waited to see the effects of the missiles' impact, but that was not to be the case.

The F-117 Stealth Fighter, having already detected the surface-to-air missile battery's radar signals, turned sharply to the left and began to arc around to intercept the missiles. She couldn't take the time, in this situation, to see if the missiles were heat seekers or radar guided.

She looked at the number of them coming up and knew she had to act quickly. This running interference was starting to get on her nerves a little, however, she remained calm and swung in behind the plane that Michael was flying.

Once she was into position, she adjusted her airspeed to be just slightly slower than the aircraft she was protecting. She then turned on the system for deploying her flare and chaff charges. Grabbing the stick tightly, she swung a wide side-to-side arc behind the plane and started dropping the flare and chaff charges. She prayed that the surface-to-air missiles, or what she was taught were called SAM's in flight training school, would take to the charges. She dropped down a little ways to see the effects of her droppings.

The surface-to-air missiles attacked the flares and chaff charges with ease. The airplane continued on its way out of Lenoran airspace. As the F-117 pilot swung the plane back up behind the aircraft, her alarm system went off as two missiles came from out of the sun, heading towards the ground.

She looked up above her and saw the plane that had fired those two missiles and she knew that those missiles where called Heat and Radiation Seeking Missiles or what she knew were known as HARM missiles. The missiles reached two other active SAM sites before they could fire. Looking down at her radar, the situation was getting worse.

"Little birdie to Red Bird One, Little birdie to Red Bird One, come in, over," she said.

"This is Red Bird One, go ahead, Little birdie," she responded.

"We have bad, bad company coming in at the two and four o'clock positions. I am in need of assistance."

"We're right here behind you. We will intercept these turkeys. Prepare for air-to-air missile defense."

"Yes, ma'am," she said, terminating the conversation and checking her plane out.

She had a few air-to-air missiles of her own as well as some air-to-ground missiles. She knew the air-to-ground missiles would be no good in an air-to-air confrontation. She looked down at her map and saw that they had little more than 20 nautical miles left before they were in friendly airspace. She flew up alongside the plane and looked into the cockpit. Michael saw her and smiled.

"Bill, it looks like we have company," said Michael, pointing over to the F-117.

"Yes, we sure do. But, how do we communicate with no radio?" asked Bill.

"I have an idea. Do we have large pens or markers and paper?" asked Michael.

"I hear you, I'll go get some."

Bill left the cockpit and returned a short time later with the large markers he found in the desk in the office part of the plane. He then set those down in his lap as he fastened his seatbelt once more. Michael looked over at the pilot of the fighter and waved.

She looked back at him and he made a sign of pointing to his ears several times and then a cross cut action back and forth across his throat. She knew then that the radio was inoperative. This situation was getting worse. She looked down at the number of aircraft and prepared to take action.

She veered off and flew a wide arc around the bottom of the plane. She turned on her missile system and started targeting the other fighters. Since they were slower and older, the missiles, she determined, weren't going to have too much trouble shooting them down. She received a positive target lock on one of the planes and pushed the button. The missile left its pod and blasted one of the Mig-29's into many pieces.

The other two pilots, seeing this happen to their comrade, veered away and came at the plane in different directions. They both fired missiles at the plane. She flew over the top of the plane that Michael was flying from wingtip to wingtip, dropping both flare and chaff charges.

As the missiles went after those once again, she switched off her targeting system only to see one Mig-29 fighter pilot heading directly at her. She realized that this pilot had no intention of turning. She switched her targeting system back on and activated her eyepiece inside her helmet.

The F-117's 20mm cannon was activated. She started shooting at the other plane and managed to hit it several times. The pilot, not bothering to eject, went down with his plane into the desert. She followed the smoke trail briefly, then returned to the rear position of the plane a few hundred meters behind. She saw the tail section and then slowed her airspeed down. She went back to being on the lookout for any more fighters, when alarms started going off.

The alarms indicated that an entire squadron of planes was headed her way. She knew what they were trying to do, cut her off. She turned on her radio and called the colonel. She looked down at the distance that they had left to fly before arriving into friendly airspace, 10 more nautical miles.

"Little birdie to Red Bird One, Little birdie to Red Bird One," she said.

"Go ahead, Little birdie, this is Red Bird One."

"I have really pissed them off. I have 14 incoming aircraft and I'm getting low on air-to-air missiles."

"You're doing a great job, Little birdie, at keeping them busy. How much further do you still have to fly to friendly airspace?" the colonel asked.

"Eight nautical miles."

"What is your airspeed?"

"565 knots. The other plane is traveling at an estimated 575 knots."

"Good, you will be in friendly airspace in just a few minutes. How close are those planes?"

"Four nautical miles and closing."

"Don't worry, they can't get to you or the plane before you're out of their airspace. Keep on flying and good luck."

"Yes, ma'am, however, their radio doesn't work."

"How do you know?"

"I flew up beside on their left side and the guy flying the plane gave me the signal of the radio not working."

"That's going to cause a problem. If they can't communicate, then how do we tell them where to fly?"

"I don't know."

"Stay with them until I can figure out how to deal with this new problem."

"Yes, ma'am, and we are in friendly airspace."

"That's good news. Please standby."

"Yes, ma'am."

Meanwhile, Michael and Bill were looking at the marker and the pad of paper. The marker, even if the letters were as large as could be made, wouldn't be large enough to be seen well. Michael looked at Bill and both of them were now wondering if they had jumped into the fire from the frying pan. When Bill had set the letters down in his lap, he looked up at Michael.

"Michael, you do realize that when we enter the restricted airspace around Spain, France, Italy, Greece etc. that, without radio communications from us, they will shoot us down."

"I know. Bill, how stupid of me," said Michael.

"What's going on?"

"Bill, is there an electrical outlet in the office?"

"Yes, on the wall next to the desk, why?"

"Bill, we still have the cell phone, right?"

"Yes, but it's dead. I see, plug it into the wall. Who are we going to call?"

"Strategic Air Command."

"I'm on it."

Bill departed and found the cell phone. After locating the charger and plugging it into the wall, he plugged the cord into the bottom of the cell phone. Bill had to wait until the power light came on before checking it over. He then dialed the phone number for Strategic Air Command Base in Nebraska. As the phone rang, he waited.

Meanwhile, the news of the radio problem had been forwarded to General Delmonte, via Colonel Minetz. He was informed of the situation and called the President to let him know that everyone was safe for the moment, however, there was a new situation.

The radio wasn't working for whatever reason and this meant lots of trouble. The President thought about it for a moment and then issued some orders to the general.

"General, that plane has to safely land in Naples, Italy. The hospital there is on the alert for her and is waiting at the airport. I understand your concern about the radio not working. Here's what I want you to do, make sure that State Department Six is ESCORTED all the way to the ground."

"Yes, Sir."

"Now, if you will excuse me, I have some commendations to type up and sign," said the President, hanging up the phone.

Meanwhile, the cell phone, although working, was not reaching anyone at Strategic Air Command Base in Nebraska. Bill stopped using the phone and left it sitting on the desktop as he walked forward. When he had closed the door to the cockpit, he spoke to Michael.

"Michael, I can't get through to anyone at Strategic Air Command Base," said Bill, rather disgustedly.

"That's a little strange. Well, we still have our escort," said Michael, pointing out the left window at the single F-117 Stealth Fighter.

"Amazing plane, isn't it, the F-117 Stealth Fighter," remarked Bill as he looked out the left window.

"Bill, keep trying to reach Strategic Air Command Base."

"Sure."

Meanwhile, General Delmonte was talking with Colonel Minetz about the situation. The general impressed upon her the need for resourceful actions by her fighter pilot. This was due to the critically wounded person aboard the airplane who was on life support. The conversation wasn't going well.

"General, my pilot cannot stay up much longer. She will be running out of fuel shortly," said Colonel Minetz.

"I understand, colonel. Has she done an in-air refueling?" asked the general.

"Only in the simulator, sir."

"Very well. I want to talk with this pilot of yours, colonel, if that is okay with you."

"I'll patch you through, general."

The captain was flying alongside State Department Six when the call came in over her radio. She answered the call signs correctly and waited to see who it was who wanted to talk to her. The voice wasn't recognizable, but the name she remembered belonged to someone who was a Joint Chiefs of Staff member.

"Good morning, captain. I understand that you are currently alongside State Department Six, is that correct?" he asked her.

"That is correct. May I ask who you are, sir?"

"I'm General Delmonte, Joint Chiefs of Staff. Listen closely to what I have to tell you. These orders are from the Commander-In-Chief himself."

"Yes, sir."

"You are to stay with State Department Six all the way to Naples, Italy. You are further ordered by the CINC to stay with the plane until it lands."

"Yes, sir, I understand the modification to my orders. However, I will not make it to Naples, Italy, sir. I am almost out of fuel."

"I understand. Have you ever done an in-air refueling?"

"No, sir, not an actual one, just the ones in the simulator."

"Okay. Where do you think you will need an in-air refueling?"

"Somewhere over the Mediterranean at or about position Tango-Six or Tango-Seven, sir."

"I understand. Standby for new orders modification."

"Yes, sir."

Meanwhile, Bill had managed to get through to Strategic Air Command Base in Nebraska. Bill explained to the person who he was and where he was located. The man at the other end was a little skeptical that Bill was who he claimed he was. The man put Bill on hold and called the base Command Duty Officer, Lieutenant Colonel Baston.

"Sorry to bother you, colonel,"

"That's okay, major, what can I do for you?"

"I have some joker on the phone who says he is Bill Yancy of the State Department and that he is aboard State Department Six," said Major Ramos.

"Can you tell me the phone number he is calling from?" asked the lieutenant colonel.

"Yes, sir. The number on my screen shows up as 202-959-2240 and the name on the screen comes up simply as 'State Department'."

"Very well, put them through to me. I'll find out if it's a joke or not."

The major put the call through to the lieutenant colonel. After the lieutenant colonel had determined who Bill was by code clearance verification, he transferred the call to General Delmonte. General Delmonte recognized Bill's voice.

"Bill, where the hell are you?" he asked.

"The last time I left the cockpit, we were at 13,333.3 meters, at a speed of 580 knots and we have an escort."

"I know. Let me give you the situation, as I know it. You are to fly to Naples, Italy, immediately. A trauma team is waiting on the ground for you and you have been given priority clearance when landing, after Naples has picked you up on radar. You will be losing your escort for a little bit while she goes and refuels. Once this is accomplished, the plane will return to your side and escort you the rest of the way."

"You do understand that our radio is not working, right?"

"Yes, that is why you have an escort."

"Thank you, General Delmonte, for your hospitality."

"You're welcome and a good job to your SPOT agent who pulled off this extraction."

"I'll pass the information along."

"Oh, by the way, have the pilot locate the emergency buttons on the left side of his seat. Have him push the button that is facing the front of the plane. This will allow him to send, via the transponders on the airplane, a silent message declaring an in-flight emergency."

"I will pass that information along as well. Thank you, sir."

Bill hung up the phone and set the phone back into the charger. He went forward to tell Michael what the general had said. As Michael listened, he said a few silent prayers for Everett in the back.

CHAPTER 8

▼

General Delmonte arranged for the in-air refueling. When the arrangements were finalized, he told the crew of the modified Boeing 707 tanker that the pilot had never done an in-air refueling outside of the simulator. They said they understood the complexity of the mission and said they would do their best. The pilot and co-pilot just looked at each other.

"Jesus Christ, no in-air refueling except in a simulator?" said the pilot.

"That's scary, sir. I might suggest that we try and keep this plane as level as possible."

"Will do. Refueling Officer, please make sure that the refueling takes place without any problems," said the pilot.

"Yes, sir. However, if that plane bumps us, we are all going down in a nice, cozy fireball," replied the refueling officer.

"I know."

When the general completed that call, he called Colonel Minetz back.

"Colonel Minetz, put me back on the air with that pilot of yours."

"Yes, General Delmonte."

There was some silence before the pilot answered the call. She turned her head so that she could hear the general better. After she showed that she was ready to listen, she engaged the autopilot.

"Captain, I understand that outside of the simulator, you have never completed an in-air refueling."

"Yes, sir that is correct. In fact, I'm getting very low on fuel at this time."

"Don't panic, remain calm. Your in-air refueling will take place over the Southern Mediterranean Sea. Your tanker is a modified Boeing 707 that has been reclassified as a BC-130."

"I understand, sir. What is my search vector?"

"Your search vector will be Tango-Seven at bearing 300."

"Got it, sir."

"Now, I have informed the crew that you have never completed an in-air refueling. They will guide you through the process just like in the simulator."

"Yes, sir."

"I want you to remain calm and change your radio frequency to 121.55 megahertz."

"I will, sir."

"Good luck."

Meanwhile, Michael had programmed the plane's new destination into the computer. The plane's computer automatically adjusted for the new point of landing in Naples, Italy. The computer offered a tip to Michael with an arrow pointing slightly northwest on a course of 300 degrees.

Michael turned the controls to the left and the plane started turning towards the new course. At that same time, the escort plane departed heading for the refueling point.

When the plane had settled onto its new course, the computer informed Michael that a course correction to 325 degrees would be needed in one hour. Michael acknowledged the course correction suggestion and put the plane back on autopilot. With the plane back on autopilot, Michael sat back in the pilot's seat and started to think. Bill could tell something was bothering Michael so he spoke to him.

"Michael, what's on your mind?" asked Bill casually.

"I've put the whole puzzle together with the exception of a few pieces and none of the theories I have fit the pieces."

"Maybe I can help."

"Bill, how many people knew about the Secretary of State being aboard this airplane?"

"Just about the entire nation courtesy of our media."

"I figured that one out. What I mean is, how many people knew where the plane was going and what the flight path would be?"

"At least five that I know of, right off the top of my head."

"Now, factor this into the equation, how many of them knew about me?"

"Two knew about you."

"And out of that two, how many knew I would probably come after Everett, you and the diplomats?"

"Still two."

"The Assistant Director of the CIA and the Assistant Secretary of State, right?"

"Yes. Michael, are you suggesting that we were sold out?"

"I have a strong suspicion of that very issue. However, from that list of two, who would have benefited from Everett's, yours and those diplomats demise?"

"A lot of people in the terrorist world."

"Right and how many people knew the flight plans of this flight?"

"The Federal Aviation Administration and us."

"You see where I'm going with this, Bill."

"Yes, I do. Michael, did anything happen before you were called in for this extraction mission?"

"A few things."

"Like what kind of things?"

"I was attacked in my apartment the day BEFORE you were claimed to have been missing. The attackers were African males and their fingerprints matched up to an INTERPOL file that had been started on them."

"What country were they from?"

"Lenora. Which means, if no one else knew the EXACT flight plans of this airplane, then someone aboard here must have revealed the flight plans."

"But why and who?"

"The why is easy to explain. You, Everett and the others were going to be paraded around in front of a camera in order for a terrorist nation to use you all as bargaining chips."

"Okay, I'll buy that. Now, who is responsible?"

"All the diplomats in the back, back there and the Assistant Director of the CIA, the Secretary of the Department of Transportation, the Director of the Federal Aviation Administration and the Assistant Secretary of State."

"Michael, you said that you were attacked the day BEFORE we went missing. Who told you that we were missing?"

"I received a phone call from your secretary. She told me some men from the CIA were in your office wanting to talk to me. I went to your office and found out who they were."

"Who told you they were the CIA?"

"Your secretary did, when she called me. Why?"

"When you went to my office, did you check their ID's?"

"Yes. The picture matched the face and the title, what are you getting at, Bill?"

"If I showed you a picture of the Director of the CIA would you recognize him?"

"Yes."

Bill left the cockpit and returned with a photo from the desktop. The picture was of the current director of the CIA, Bill, Everett and three other persons, from a few years earlier. Bill showed the photo to Michael who became very alarmed.

"Bill, that's not the man I spoke with in your office that day. However, the man standing to your right, his identification checked out as Marcos Sanchez, the Assistant Director of the CIA."

"That name and face is correct. I'm curious, do you remember the name that the other man gave to you?"

"Yes, he gave me the name of Roger Smith."

"Roger Smith? Now, that's interesting."

"Why is that interesting, Bill?"

"Roger Smith is a very good friend of mine. He is also an agent for the National Security Agency."

"Why would this person lie to me?"

"I don't know. Michael, would you recognize this man who was obviously masquerading as someone else if you saw him again?"

"Yes, I am reasonably certain of that."

"Good. When we get back to the United States, I'm going to start asking questions and hopefully get some answers. By the way, were you attacked the same day as my reported disappearance?"

"Yes, why?"

"Michael, I think you may be right about the being sold out theory. Not many people knew we were missing until probably a couple of days later."

"Bill, I think that one of those diplomats back there sold you all out."

"Who?"

"Which one of those diplomats is from an African country that has a common border with Lenora?"

"I see what you mean. But why try and kill Everett?"

"I think that was an accident. Answer this question, did anyone ever interrogate or torture you?"

"No, just Everett getting shot in the back."

"Then I think that diplomat may have been the one thing that kept you all alive."

"I see what you're saying."

"Bill, don't talk to anybody about this until we have further proof."

"I hear you. Are you going to do some fact-finding of your own?"

"Yes."

The computer tripped an alarm telling Michael that it was time to turn the plane to the new course of 325 degrees. Michael first acknowledged the alarm and then turned the wheel until the compass reading was 325 degrees. When this was completed, Michael reengaged the autopilot and they both flew in silence. They were so absorbed by their newfound revelations, that neither one of them noticed the escort plane return alongside them.

Suddenly things went terribly wrong aboard the plane. The one diplomat injured the other two and then forced his way into the cockpit. In the ensuing fight, the plane's autopilot was disengaged. The plane started to drop altitude quickly.

As Michael and Bill fought the diplomat, the diplomat pulled out a gun, which had been hidden inside his jacket. Michael grabbed the gun and turned it into the diplomat who fired several times into himself. As the dead diplomat was slumping to the floor, Michael looked at the altimeter.

The plane was heading for the surface of the Mediterranean Sea.

Michael regained the controls and started climbing back up to their previous altitude. Once the autopilot had been reengaged, the plane leveled off, Michael turned to Bill.

"Bill, check on the others," Michael said.

"Right away," said Bill, as he stepped over the body of the diplomat.

Bill checked the other diplomats out. They were okay with the exception of Everett. The diplomat had damaged the battery power pack and it was dying much faster. Bill looked at the monitors, which showed she was near death.

Her blood oxygen content was at 18 percent; her heart rate had slowed down to just 35 beats a minute. Her blood pressure was low as well. From Bill's point of view, her whole body had taken on a blue tinge on the skin. Bill looked at the acid dripping onto the deck of the plane from the damaged battery power pack and cursed at himself. Walking forward, he stepped over the body and rejoined Michael as copilot.

"That diplomat damaged Everett's life support machine. I don't know how much longer it will last," Bill said.

"That son of a bitch. If she dies, then I hope he goes to hell."

Bill was getting ready to say something, when the cell phone rang. He exited the cockpit and answered the phone. He found out it was Strategic Air Command Base on a live link to them with General Delmonte.

"Bill, what's going on up there? My escort said you dropped almost 7,000 meters before returning to your previous altitude."

"We had a problem with one of the diplomats. Look, I would like to explain everything, but we have a new problem."

"What's that?"

"The problem diplomat damaged Everett's life support system. I don't think the battery power pack will remain operable much longer. Since I don't have any more battery packs, the unit will shut off and she will suffocate."

"I understand. Naples, Italy tower is telling me that they still don't have you on their screens yet. However, when you do show up on their screens, they are telling me to tell you to land on runway 27 left."

"I hear you, sir."

"Stay by the phone, Naples trauma team will be contacting you shortly. They will want Everett's vital signs, etc."

"I'll be waiting, sir."

Michael waited patiently for Bill to return. When Bill returned, he stepped over the body and spoke to Michael. Michael turned to look at him with grave concern in his eyes.

"Michael, I have to go sit by Everett. General Delmonte says that the Naples trauma team will be calling shortly."

"That sounds great, Bill. But we may have another problem."

"What's that?"

"I counted the number of rounds fired to the number of bullet holes in the man's body. There is one round unaccounted for," said Michael pointing at the copilot's seat where he had unloaded the man's weapon.

"Where did that round go?"

"I don't know. I don't think it exited the skin of the airplane or else we would be dead already. Bill, was the cockpit door open or closed during the fight?"

"Open. I see what you mean," Bill said, as he hurried back to check on the other diplomats.

"Gentlemen, would you all mind taking off your jackets and shirts and pants. I need to check for a bullet."

The one diplomat stood up, rather shakily, and looked right at Bill.

"There will be no need for that, Mr. Yancy. The bullet you are looking for is in my right ass cheek and it hurts very badly."

"Remain calm, I will get the first aid kit. Sir, would you make sure that he is placed face down on the couch there?" asked Bill of the other diplomat, pointing at a small couch.

"I will take care of my friend here. Please bring me the first aid kit."

Bill left and returned with a first aid kit. After dropping the kit off, he returned to the cockpit. He was trying very hard not to laugh, but the smile and inflated cheeks gave him away. Michael turned around and started chuckling as well.

"Bill, what's so funny?" asked Michael.

"The missing bullet is in the one diplomat's right ass cheek."

"Oh, I see, well, I bet you that smarts."

"Yes, it does. Good luck, Michael."

Bill was walking passed the desk, when the cell phone started to ring. He picked it up and noticed that it had at least a partial charge on the batteries. He answered the phone as he was heading towards the rear of the plane. The Naples trauma team's leading doctor was on the other end of the line. Bill had just stepped into the medical area and closed the door behind himself.

"Yes, doctor what can I do for you?" asked Bill.

"First of all, how many wounded do you have?" he asked.

"Two. One critically and the other non critically."

"Okay, got it. Now, the one critically wounded, by what means, etc."

"Gunshot wound to the back. The bullet entered the left side of the back almost right between the shoulder blades."

"Did the bullet exit?"

"No, it is still in there."

"Is the wound oozing any blood?"

"No, in fact, the wound has started to heal over. I see no fresh blood."

"That's good. What are the critically wounded person's vitals?"

"Her life support machine is about to die. Someone intentionally damaged it. There's battery acid leaking all over the deck of the plane."

"I understand. I don't want you to panic. What are the rest of the vitals?"

"Heart rate is 30 beats a minute, blood pressure 70 over 85, blood oxygen content 19 percent."

"Okay, I got all that information. On the second wounded, what are their vitals?"

"Oh, they're alright. They're complaining about being face down with their ass stuck up in the air," replied Bill.

"That's good enough for me. Where is the wound at and what type of wound is it?"

"The wound is a bullet wound in the person's right ass cheek."

"I got that information. Both parties will be treated upon arrival.

Bill, tell me where the energy indicator is at on the life support machine."

"It is in the low end of the yellow area about to enter the red zone."

"I understand. Bill, please tell the pilot that upon landing, they cannot use the flaps for stopping. The sudden compression force might stop Everett's heart. Do you understand?"

"Yes, I understand."

"Bill, can you by any chance plug the life support machine into the wall outlet?"

"No, the cord has been cut into several pieces."

"Okay, please standby."

Bill shut off the phone and walked out of the medical ward of the plane. He kept the cell phone with him this time. He stopped by the one diplomat and told him that the medical team would assist him when they landed. Bill continued going forward until he stepped into the cockpit. Michael turned around to face him.

"I heard the cell phone ring, Bill."

"You're right and the doctor passed along something to me that sounds rather bad."

"What's that?"

"Due to Everett's vital signs being so bad, he said you can't use the flaps on landing because the sudden compression might stop her heart."

"I understand. Bill, tell everyone back there to buckle up, this is going to be an ugly landing."

"I will and pray that Everett's life support machine doesn't fail before we land."

"What's wrong with it?"

"The battery power pack was destroyed, remember? Besides, the cord was cut into several pieces."

"Bill, I'm not about to give up, let me have a look."

"Okay."

Michael left the cockpit and went to see Everett. He saw the machine was slowing down. He looked at the deck of the plane and saw where the battery acid was slowly eating a hole in the deck. As he looked at the cut pieces of the power cord, he noticed that there was a small piece of the power cord still left.

He looked around the medical area. There, sitting on the deck, was an extension cord. Grabbing the extension cord, he walked out of the medical area and into the cockpit.

"Here's our answer, Bill," said Michael, tossing the extension cord into Bill's lap.

"But the wires are cut off of her machine. How is this going to help?"

"Bill, look behind me on the deck of the plane. You see that hatch?" asked Michael, pointing to the top of the hatch.

"Yes," he replied.

"Go down into the forward cargo hold. In there, on the right side of the plane, you will find a toolbox. Look inside the toolbox for some wire cutters and either small twist caps or electrical tape. Bring them to me."

"I'll check it out."

Bill opened the hatch and went down inside the cargo hold. Once he was down there, he found the toolbox and brought the entire thing up to Michael. Michael dumped out the contents of the toolbox onto the floor of the forward galley.

Inside the pile, Michael found what he was looking for and made the extension cord into a makeshift electrical plug and cord. When the final piece was taped off, Michael plugged the cord into the wall socket next to the desk and the life support machine switched over to main power immediately.

Michael returned to the cockpit and rubbed his eyes. He was starting to get tired. At the same time he was getting tired, he looked up and saw something wonderful in the cockpit instruments above him.

A pull switch with the words EMERGENCY BRAKING SYSTEM located under it. As he looked at those words, he wondered what kind of emergency breaking system a plane like this could have. When Bill stepped back into the cockpit, Michael turned around to look at him.

CHAPTER 9

▼

"Bill, what does the emergency braking system consist of on this aircraft?" asked Michael.

"Oh, in case of a failure of the brake system, a series of parachutes are deployed out the back to slow the aircraft down. At the same time, the engines are shutdown to a low level and reverse rockets are activated. Why?"

"I found out how we can land without using the landing flaps."

"Michael, that system has never actually been used. In fact, there are some unconfirmed reports that this system may not work at all."

"Well, I guess instead of a test, we will give the system its first actual job. Pray that this system will stop this plane slowly. By the way, how are our two diplomats getting along?"

"When I last left them, they were discussing trade agreements between their countries. That hasn't happened at all in the last 20 years."

"Well, at least the trip wasn't totally fruitless."

Suddenly, all sorts of alarms and lights went off in the cockpit. Michael looked down at the readouts and the readouts told him the plane had entered the outer edge of the Naples, Italy airspace.

Michael silenced the alarms and took the plane off of autopilot. He had been told to land on runway 27 left and that's the direction he pointed the plane. As they began their descent, they ran into turbulence.

The whole plane started shaking and shuddering from one end to the other. A door to the aft galley that had not been secured came open and dumped its contents out onto the galley floor.

Cups, plastic wares and silverware rained down on the galley deck making a lot of noise. Bill looked up and went back to check out the noise. He returned with the report of the door not being closed.

As the plane descended further, the turbulence increased. By the time Michael passed the 6,000-meter mark, the turbulence had started to subside. When Michael passed the 3,000-meter mark, the turbulence had ceased. Leveling off after this heavy turbulence was great. As Bill sat next to Michael in the copilot's seat, Michael discussed his landing plans with him.

"Bill, once we touchdown, I want you to stand on the brake pedal while I activate the emergency breaking system. Since Everett is closet to the rear door, standby there when we come to a halt."

"Will do."

Another set of alarms went off; Michael acknowledged them and looked down at the digital displays. The flight computer was telling Michael he was over the outer marker for the airport. Another alarm indicated that the plane was over the outer marker for runway 27 left.

Although Michael couldn't see it, trouble was brewing in Everett's machine. Sparks were flying from the exposed wire from the life support machine rubbing up against the wall during all the turbulence. Suddenly there was a fire.

Michael and Bill were going over the landing procedures when the uninjured diplomat came up to the cockpit. He went to knock on the cockpit door, but found it open instead. He knocked on the open door. Bill turned around to see who it was.

"Yes, sir, what can I do for you?" asked Bill.

"I smell something burning, Mr. Yancy."

"Sit back down in your seat and fasten your seatbelt. I will check it out."

"Yes, sir."

The diplomat and Bill walked back towards the rear of the aircraft. Even before Bill reached the medical room, he could see something coming out from under the door. Cautiously he approached the door and felt it, it was still cool but, now, smoke was visible, coming out from underneath the door. Closing his eyes and then opening them again, he opened the door and was attacked by the flames from the fire.

He quickly closed the door and grabbed a fire extinguisher from the galley and reopened the door. Working quickly, he extinguished the flames and then waited a few more minutes before putting the empty fire extinguisher on the deck. He then returned to the cockpit, smoke-filled clothing and all. As he took his seat, he buckled his seatbelt.

"I'm glad you're here, I just passed over the inner marker. I have visual on the runway. Is something on fire?" asked Michael, sniffing the air.

"Yes, there was a fire in the medical area."

"Oh my God, is the fire out?!"

"Yes. How much longer before we land?"

"About five minutes."

Michael pushed a button and the landing gear deployed. Pushing the control stick down a little further, the plane started descending further. When the plane touched down, Michael looked out the windows to see emergency equipment chasing the plane and several ambulances at the very end of the runway.

While Bill stepped as hard as he could on the brake pedal, Michael deployed the parachutes out the back. The plane glided to a stop effortlessly at the very end of the runway where Michael noticed nothing but weeds, tall grass and the painted "V" lines showing where the runway ended.

Michael quickly shut the engines the rest of the way down and met the medical crew at the back of the airplane. The medical crew took Everett first and then took the other injured party. The crew then divided up and took the body off the plane. Michael, Bill and the other diplomat were escorted off the plane and once they were on the ground, Michael had a chance to see the escort plane parked right next to them. After the plane was refueled, the plane took off and disappeared into the afternoon sky.

Bill and Michael were taken to the military hospital where Everett was getting prepped for surgery. The trauma team's senior doctor looked over the X-rays and didn't like what he saw. He put the X-rays down and called for the Chief of the Trauma Unit's Neurological surgeon. The surgeon arrived shortly and began looking at the X-rays. It wasn't until the surgeons were in surgery that they discovered how much damage had been done by the bullet.

The bullet had nicked the vertebrae and had splintered the bone tissue. The neurological surgeon looked at it, but didn't find any direct damage to the spinal cord itself. He used bone chips from her hips to fuse into temporary vertebrae.

When this had been completed, the damage to her rib bone and lung was repaired. When the surgery was done, she was sent to the recovery room and the neurological surgeon met with Michael and Bill to discuss her condition.

"Everett is an amazingly tough woman, Mr. Pigeon. Now, I repaired the damage done by the bullet. However, there is high probability that her spinal cord was damaged," said the surgeon.

"You mean she is paralyzed?" asked Michael.

"Could be paralyzed. I don't know and I won't know for a few more days. Mr. Yancy, if either you or Mr. Pigeon could stay here until she can be transported back to the United States, that would be a great help to her."

"Well, Michael, I do have some business to conduct back in the U.S.; why don't you stay here with her," said Bill, winking his left eye at Michael.

"I would be happy to stay here. Where can I stay doctor?" asked Michael.

"She's in intensive care right now. There's a hotel down the road, in fact, it's within walking distance."

"Thank you very much. Doctor, can I see her for just a few minutes?" asked Michael as Bill was heading towards the elevator.

"Sure, she's in room A223."

"Thanks."

Michael walked into the room and saw her lying there, face down with the breathing tube coming out of her mouth. The machine next to her bed whooshed up and down to aid her breathing. He walked over to her bedside and sat with her for a few minutes before leaving to get his hotel room.

By the evening, she had started coming out of the anesthesia and opened her eyes to find Michael sitting at her bedside. She blinked her eyes to help clear them up and then when she was sure that Michael was looking at her, she winked her right eye.

Michael was able to stay with her for the next several days. This worked out nicely for Bill's plans. He was preparing the inquiry into who was masquerading as whom in his office. He didn't blame Michael for taking on the mission, but he did blame him for not doing a more thorough job on checking everyone's story out as to who they were. As he finished typing up the request, he printed it off on the printer and then faxed it on his secure fax machine to the headquarters of the National Security Agency.

One day, Michael was sitting by Everett's bedside when she woke up and looked at him with both eyes wide open. She looked like she was going to say something, then fell back down onto the bed. When the doctor came in, Michael asked him about that observation.

"She was probably having a flashback to the shooting. This is quite common in gunshot victims. She probably will have these flashbacks for the rest of her life. Now, has she even tried to move her legs at all?" asked the neurological specialist.

"No, not yet. She is fatigued so easily, why?"

"She lost a lot of blood. When the body looses this amount of blood, it can take weeks or months to replace it. During that time, the amount of oxygen carrying blood is reduced. Therefore, all the cells in the body are on a wait and see type system."

"Is there anything that can be done?"

"Time is the only thing that will take care of that. However, if she wants to try and walk or turn herself over in bed, then I can prescribe a drug called EPO to help with that issue."

"Please do whatever you can. Is she going somewhere today?"

"Yes, I need to take her down to the MRI scanner. I want to take some pictures of her spine where the bullet entered. I need to check the healing progress of the bone chips that I fused into her back."

"Okay, madam Secretary Everett, do you need any help in this matter?" asked Michael.

"Sure, I could use a little help," she replied with a slightly hoarse voice from the breathing tube that had been removed earlier in the morning.

Michael, the doctor and the two orderlies helped put Everett into the wheelchair. They took her down to the magnetic resonance imaging machine and placed her on the table. The doctor left the orders on the tabletop for the MRI nurse to process. She picked up the orders and programmed the computer with the orders and the table moved Everett inside the machine. For the next hour and half, she was inside the machine. When the MRI was completed, the nurse, Michael and the two orderlies put her into the wheelchair.

Michael put her into her bed and she started to cry. Michael laid her down and then looked at her. She handed Michael the do's and don'ts list and Michael found something humorous on the list of things not to do for the next couple of weeks.

"Madam Secretary, it says here you are not to engage in stressful or aggressive sex," said Michael.

"Oh, gee, I'm glad you told me that one. I'll have to remember that one when I'm at the next Washington D.C. gala," she said and smiled for the first time since waking up from the surgery.

It wasn't until a few days later that the results came back on the MRI. The neurological surgeon looked at the wound that day. After taking some measurements, he asked Everett how her appetite was and a bunch of other questions before leaving the room.

That afternoon, an orthopedics specialist came into the room and had Everett perform a lot of different resistance exercises. After this was completed, she was totally exhausted and fell asleep almost immediately. Michael was summoned to the outside of her room.

"Mr. Pigeon, she has good resistance and good dexterity for someone who has had this type of spinal surgery repair. However, I found some things on the MRI that I don't like. There is a possibility that she could be paralyzed forever if she moves the wrong way," said the orthopedic surgeon.

"I understand, but I want you to think about this. She never gave up on me and hung on to the smallest thread of life. She went beyond what a normal human could have tolerated before giving up. She didn't give up, so neither should you," proclaimed Michael.

"I hear you, Mr. Pigeon. If her tests in the morning come back favorable, I can let her have more time with you alone. I have seen the way you two act, you're a very positive force for her," said the neurological surgeon.

"Don't forget what I said," Michael reminded them before he left them standing in the hallway entering into her room.

She tried to sit up, but was very exhausted from the effort. She was crying once again. Michael waited until the door was shut before going over and comforting her. Her eyes were full of tears and she was almost choking on her own saliva.

All she could do was hug Michael. The only noises were her crying and the air conditioner running behind him. When she had fallen asleep, Michael was getting ready to go down to the hospital cafeteria for lunch when the phone rang in her room. Michael reached over her to answer it before the noise woke her up.

"Michael Pigeon," he said.

"Michael, it's Bill. Look, you were more right than you know about being sold out. It appears that my report with your questions that you wanted answers to was sent back to me this morning from the National Security Agency."

"What were the answers?"

"I can't tell you over the phone. When can you get back to Denver?"

"Let me get a status check on Everett before I leave."

"Get back here as quickly as possible, it may be worse than we thought."

"I understand," replied Michael, hanging up the phone.

He looked down at Everett and saw that she was still asleep. He walked down the hallway and then ate lunch in the hospital cafeteria. When he returned, he found Everett eating her lunch. He started smiling and sat down in the chair next to her bed. When she had finished off her lunch, she turned herself over slightly in bed to face Michael.

"Bill called you earlier, is everything alright?" she asked.

"Yes and no. Madam Secretary, you and your diplomatic friends were sold out by someone in order to help either terrorists or terrorist organizations gain a huge foothold on the U.S."

"Why?"

"You and your friends were going to be used as bargaining chips."

"Oh Lord, what went wrong?"

"I think they were counting on eliminating me before I received your phone call to come get you. You see, I was attacked the day

BEFORE you were reported missing, by two Lenoran males. Then some odd things started happening."

"I see. Does Bill want you to return to Denver to help him?"

"Yes, but I told him I wasn't leaving until I received a favorable report or your official release."

"Well, I will let you go back to Denver under one condition."

"What's that?"

"I want you to have sex with me before you go."

"You know the doctors and the nurses aren't going to like that very much."

"No, but the amount of endorphins released during sex is a lot better, and probably cheaper than the painkillers they are giving me now."

"You do have a point there. Okay, as long as it is not aggressive or stressful sex."

Michael went down to the nurses' station and made arrangements for the act to happen. The nurses down there were concerned, but they agreed that it probably wouldn't hurt her as long as it wasn't aggressive sex. Michael returned to the room and closed the curtain around the bed.

When Everett had drifted off to sleep, Michael left the room and went to his hotel room. He packed up and went to the airport where he was able to get aboard a flight to the United States via London, England on standby space availability. Once in London, he was able to get a late night flight to the United States and was soon landing in Denver, Colorado just a little after 1000 hours. He went immediately to Bill's office and closed the door behind himself.

Bill looked at Michael and wondered when the last time he had slept was. Michael looked at Bill and smiled as best he could. Michael was tired and exhausted from the long flight to the United States. When Michael looked up the next time at Bill, Bill was handing Michael a stack of paperwork. The paperwork concerned the person who was masquerading as Roger Smith of the CIA.

Michael looked at the picture and it really wasn't the Director of the CIA. Next, he looked at the report. The report detailed that Roger Smith was actually a National Security Agency operative working in the United States.

Michael turned to the next page and saw the picture of the real Roger Smith. It wasn't the man who had been standing in Bill's office that day. When Michael turned to the next page, he received the shock of his life. The picture had a red label across the picture saying: DECEASED.

"Bill, he's dead. How did a dead man appear in your office masquerading as the Director of the CIA?" asked Michael.

"I thought that it might be impossible, until I read the date of death," replied Bill.

Michael turned the picture over and saw the date. The date was the day before the plane went missing.

"You mean I was talking to a ghost?"

"No, I think someone did some very fancy makeup and face painting."

"I'm sorry, Bill. I should have checked them all out more thoroughly."

"Here's something from the CIA to you," Bill said, handing Michael a letter.

The letter stated that the Assistant Director of the CIA was at headquarters all day and could not have been in Denver, Colorado at the time estimated by your SPOT Agent Michael Pigeon. We regret any inconvenience that this may cause in your investigation.

"Holy Shit, Bill, was everyone I talked to some sort of face painted person with fake ID's?" said Michael.

"It would appear so. I have the FBI and CIA both on alert for these people. Maybe we can catch them before they pull off another stunt like this."

"I sure hope so, Bill."

The phone started ringing in Bill's office. Bill picked up the phone and handed the receiver over to Michael. He yawned and spoke into the phone. It was Everett at the other end of the line.

She just called to tell him that she loved him very much and that in a few more weeks, she would be returning to the United States. In fact, she was being flown to a premier spinal injury hospital near Boulder, Colorado. Michael was very happy and said he thought that it was great, but how did she manage to get transferred there. She told him it was something that he had said to the doctors in the hallway. Michael said goodbye and went home. For the rest of the day he slept.

CHAPTER 10

▼

For the next few days, Michael rested and reported to work whenever Bill called him. Michael was amazed at the amount of information coming in during this investigation. During one of his many days off, he went into work and picked up his Glock® Model 20. His Sixth sense was telling him of danger that was close at hand.

Before going back home, he stopped by a sporting goods store and purchased several boxes of silvertip hollow point ammunition. After loading up all five magazines, he chambered a round and replaced the round at the top of the magazine with another one before reinserting the magazine. Putting the pistol back into his shoulder holster, he drove home.

Upon arriving at home, he found some strange marks on the front door. He bent down and examined them closer and saw that they were from someone trying to break into his apartment. Finding no other marks, he unsnapped his holster and withdrew his pistol. Carefully, he opened the front door to his apartment, keeping the pistol in the close quarter combat position.

A figure moved out of the shadows at him. As the figure tried to push passed Michael, Michael was able to get a good look at the person. The person was one of the people that were supposed to be dead. Michael was able to fire twice. He hit the figure both times, but the figure kept right on going. Michael set his sights on the person again waiting for a viable target to present itself to him. The figure was getting away when Michael found a target of opportunity. The figure had to turn to get down the stairs; when he turned the corner, Michael fired twice more.

The figure momentarily stopped moving but stood right back up again. Michael was stunned by this movement of getting up after being hit with this ammunition. Michael started to doubt his own shooting abilities.

The figure was close the first time and farther the second time. Michael raced down the hallway to the end. He sprinted down the stairs to the bottom. He saw blood all over the carpet and out onto the sidewalk.

Rushing out the door and into the bitter cold, Michael looked around for some signs of where the figure had disappeared. He looked down on the sidewalk, which was partially covered in snow and started tracking the blood droplets left. In the meantime, he pulled his cell phone out and called the special SPOT Agent phone number.

He was told that several agents were being sent to the area and to be extremely careful. After hanging up the phone, he removed the partially used magazine and inserted a fresh one. He put the partially used magazine into his back pocket. He then reholstered his weapon and started to search for the figure.

When the other agents arrived, they all fanned out in a large group looking for someone with gunshot wounds. The blood trail that Michael was following suddenly stopped in a back alley. The snow was only slightly bloodstained and so Michael started cursing and swearing at himself for being led to a dead end. He was about to leave when he saw more blood on the other side of the alleyway.

Quickly, he moved towards the end of the street and noticed that the blood trail stopped once again. The trail stopped at a corner and now Michael had to determine which way the man had gone. He was on the opposite side of the street when his cell phone rang. He looked at the number and saw that it was Bill who was calling.

"Hello, Bill," said Michael.

"Michael, are you alright?"

"For the time being. However, I shot someone who had broken into my apartment. In fact, I shot this person several times and I'm not too sure that I even hit him."

"Did you recognize who you shot?"

"Yeah, and he's supposed to be dead."

"How many times did you shoot him?"

"Four all together. I think I only hit him twice though in the lower abdomen or maybe the legs."

"Michael, what's your location?"

"I'm several blocks below my apartment somewhere in the area of 84th and Bannock Streets."

"Michael, keep on this person's blood trail. I'm coming to your location. I'll be there in 30 minutes. Be careful, this doesn't sound good to me."

"I'll be waiting."

Michael hung up his cell phone and looked down in the snow. The blood trail was becoming smaller and smaller. Michael knew that the person could be either very close to where he was standing or dead by now. He continued walking slowly down the street until he came to a deserted looking apartment building.

He looked up at the building and then circled around back. Not finding any blood trail back there, he started looking carefully around the area. Finding no more blood above or on the other side of the street from this building, he was certain that person was inside the building. His cell phone rang once more.

"Hello, Bill," said Michael.

"Michael, where are you?" asked Bill.

"I'm at 8712 South Bannock Street at an abandoned apartment building."

"Okay, I'm almost there," he replied, hanging up the phone.

Bill pulled up in his car and jumped out. He signaled to Michael and Michael soon joined him at the car.

"What's going on, Michael?" asked Bill.

"The blood trail stops at this apartment building."

"There's no blood anywhere else?"

"No. I checked the back; it's clean. I checked up the street and on the other side. I even went so far as to double back on myself and didn't find any fresh blood droplets."

"You think whomever you shot is in that building?"

"Yes, I do."

"I'm calling for back-up."

Bill turned away from Michael and made a series of phone calls. All this time, the person who had been shot by Michael was watching what was going on outside the abandoned apartment building with a keen interest. When the back-up units arrived, Bill gave them their orders. Michael put on some body armor on the outside of his clothing. When everyone was starting to walk inside the building, Bill turned to face Michael.

"Are you ready?" he asked.

"We're going inside?"

"You scared, or would you prefer to keep company with the drug dealers out here?"

"We're going in," said Michael, pulling his pistol out of his holster.

"Michael, we're heading up the stairs to the top floor."

"Let's go."

Michael and Bill entered the building. On the way up the stairs, each one performed stair clearing. Once they were to the top of the stairs, they both stopped and listened. No noises could be heard, so Bill turned to Michael.

"Room clearing," said Bill.

"Right or left?"

"We will have to do both. Let's start on the right and stay out of the way of the door."

"Will do."

Bill and Michael began to systematically open doors and check the rooms out. After checking a room, Bill would shut the door and they would proceed to the next room. Bill now noticed that since the sun had gone down, it was getting dark in the hallway. Since the apartment building was abandoned, no electricity was available to power the lights in the hallway.

He pulled out a flashlight and started to use it to search the floor and the doors before entering. Michael pulled out his own penlight from his right upper shirt pocket and turned it on. When the beam from Bill's flashlight was on the doorknob of the next room, Michael saw the blood on it.

"Bill, there's blood on the doorknob," said Michael, whispering it to Bill.

Bill looked down and, sure enough, there was blood smeared all over the doorknob. Bill looked back up at Michael.

"Could be a decoy, too," said Bill.

"Kick open the door," said Michael with his pistol at the ready with the flashlight in his other hand.

Bill kicked the door open and gunfire erupted from the room. Michael started firing into the room and emptied the magazine very quickly. Bill was shooting into the room as well and stopped to reload. When the slide was shut on Michael's weapon, he turned to look at Bill.

"Bill, I'll roll into the room and provide you cover fire. Enter right afterwards," said Michael.

"Right behind you."

Michael burst into the room and rolled to a stop. In the prone position, he started firing and emptied that magazine in a short period of time. Bill was right behind him and provided him cover fire while he reloaded. Once Michael had reloaded, Bill reloaded his revolver. They looked around with their flashlights and that's when more gunfire erupted.

The bullets were coming in from the bedroom to their left. Michael fired into the doorway and into the doorframe as he advanced forward. Michael had made it to the doorway only to find his pistol failed to fire. Michael shone his light into his right hand and saw that the magazine was empty once more. Michael inserted the last fully loaded magazine into the pistol and closed the action.

Bill had reloaded his revolver and ran across the room to stand on the opposite side of where Michael was. The gunfire had temporarily ceased as the other agents, having heard gunfire, converged on that floor. One of the agents that showed up was armed with a shotgun. Michael waved him into the room.

"Fire into the room when we roll into it!" yelled Michael.

"Yes, sir."

The man thrust the barrel of the shotgun into the room and started firing. Spent shotgun shells, revolver cartridges and the smell of burnt gunpowder filled the air. Michael was wondering why the police weren't on the scene yet, and then it dawned on him, maybe they were afraid of this area. Michael and Bill burst into the room to find a dead body that was still holding a semi-automatic rifle.

Bill and Michael approached cautiously. Bill kicked the person's feet before getting any closer. Michael was looking around the room and yelled at Bill because he couldn't hear himself to begin with.

"Bill, I think this is a set up. There may be more of these people around here," yelled Michael.

"What makes you think that?" asked Bill.

Before Michael could respond, Michael saw the closet door begin to slowly open from the beam of his flashlight. Michael shoved Bill out of the way and brought his pistol to bear. The person shot Michael first as Michael was standing in the way of their escape. Michael was able to empty the partially used magazine into the person and then looked around, as the room seemed to be moving.

Michael never heard the gun go off, but he did feel the impact of the bullet into his vest. The .45 ACP round hit him square in the chest and knocked him both off of his feet and onto the floor. As the person was trying to leave, the agent with the shotgun stopped him at the doorway. The person flew backwards into Michael who was just standing back up.

This impact injured him. The breath was knocked out of him and the impact of the person's body was incredible. Michael put his right foot back and that's when he felt the pain that suddenly came over him. He looked down at his right leg and saw it twisted off to one side. Michael gasped and then passed out.

When he became aware of his surroundings, he opened his eyes. He recognized the place as a hospital emergency room. He looked over at the two persons standing to his right. Then he looked to the foot of the gurney he was on. The person at the foot of the gurney smiled.

"Mr. Pigeon, do you know where you are?" asked the orthopedic surgeon.

"Yes, I'm in what appears to be a hospital emergency room," responded Michael.

"You're quite right. Your right leg is not broken, but the X-ray did reveal that your hip is out of place. I'm going to have to put your hip back into place and it's going to hurt."

"I don't think it could possibly hurt any more than what it does right now."

"How would you rate your pain at this time on a scale of 1 to 10?"

"Plus 20."

"Well, these other two gentlemen are going to assist me in putting your hip back into place."

"When do we start?"

"Right now."

Michael noticed that the doctor gave him a huge shot of something into his left arm. The doctor left and returned with a pair of crutches and leg brace. He set them down and that's when Michael realized that his head was now swimming in the painkiller that he had been given. Michael was having a hard time concentrating on anything.

"How are you feeling right now?" asked the surgeon.

"Just fine," replied Michael.

"Well, here we go."

In a matter of seconds, the surgeon put Michael's hip back into place. The other two orderlies held Michael down for the procedure. As soon as this was completed, the surgeon left the room and Bill walked into it.

"Well, looks like you're doing quite well," snickered Bill.

"You know, in a few months I will probably laugh at this incident too. Who were those people?"

"Illegal aliens in the country. They were from Lenora and the armorer has your weapon."

"They both looked white to me. How did they do it?"

"Oxygen treatments will bleach out your skin. Why don't you take some time off?"

"Guess I will have to, now."

"I have a special surprise for you."

"What's that?"

Bill left the room and Secretary Everett appeared in the doorway. She was more beautiful than ever and she was standing up. She walked rather ungainly towards Michael's bed and then had to use the bed as a support. Michael's mouth dropped open.

"Madam Secretary Everett, you're walking," said Michael.

"A little bit each day. I am also off to my office so that I can properly discharge my duties," she said bending down and kissing him.

"Thank you, but now I'm the injured one."

"I can see that."

The surgeon came back into the room and fitted Michael for his crutches and signed his release paperwork. Bill took Everett and Michael to the airport so that Michael could see Everett off. As they were walking back to the car, Michael smiled.

He then made a silent vow to himself that he would have those jewels he had received during one of his many missions made into an engagement ring and a wedding band. Michael stepped into the car and Bill drove Michael home.